✳ Tim twisted an[d] quickly arrived at a th[icket,] ing over heavy roots and ducking under bare branches. There were dead leaves on the ground, and Tim could hear the crunching of his pursuers' feet behind him.

He put on speed. In fact, he pumped his feet so fast he never saw the net that was stretched between two bushes before it had snagged him.

"Oof!" he cried out as he tripped and stumbled, caught in his midsection by the net. He saw that two burly men in identical hats and overcoats were gripping the edges of the strong net. When he was just inches from landing facedown on the ground, a powerful hand jerked Tim's head back by his hair and held him upright. Tim gulped. He felt the cold blade of a knife at his throat.

"Keep your voice to a whisper if you know what's good for you," a deep voice said. ✳

the BOOKS of MAGIC™ *2

Bindings

Carla Jablonski

Created by
Neil Gaiman and John Bolton

BOOKS FOR
VERTIGO
YOUNG ADULTS

eos

An Imprint of HarperCollinsPublishers

Eos is an imprint of HarperCollins Publishers.

The Books of Magic 2: Bindings

The Books of Magic: Bindings comic books were created
by the following people:
Written by John Ney Rieber
Illustrated by Gary Amaro and Peter Gross

Library of Congress Cataloging-in-Publication Data
Jablonski, Carla.
   Bindings / Carla Jablonski ; created by Neil Gaiman and John Bolton.— 1st
Eos ed.
      p.   cm.
   Based on the graphic novel characters created by Neil Gaiman and illustrated by
John Bolton and others; first published in single magazine form as, "The Books of
Magic, 1–4."
   Summary: In this novelization of The Books of Magic, number two, Tim Hunter
encounters new danger and trials on his journey to become the world's greatest
practitioner of magic.
   ISBN 0-06-447380-5 (pbk.)
   [1. Magic—Fiction. 2. Occultism—Fiction.] I. Gaiman, Neil Books of Magic. II.
Bolton, John, 1951– III. Title.
PZ7.J1285 Bi 2003   2002013282
[Fic]—dc21   CIP
                                                                    AC

Typography by Henrietta Stern
❖

First Eos edition, 2003
Visit us on the World Wide Web!
www.harperteen.com
www.dccomics.com

To Rich T and Charlie K,
for making the magic happen.
—CJ

THE BOOKS OF MAGIC
An Introduction

by Neil Gaiman

Wʜᴇɴ ɪ ᴡᴀs sᴛɪʟʟ a teenager, only a few years older than Tim Hunter is in the book you are holding, I decided it was time to write my first novel. It was to be called *Wild Magic*, and it was to be set in a minor British Public School (which is to say, a private school), like the ones from which I had so recently escaped, only a minor British Public School that taught magic. It had a young hero named Richard Grenville, and a pair of wonderful villains who called themselves Mister Croup and Mister Vandemar. It was going to be a mixture of Ursula K. Le Guin's *A Wizard of Earthsea* and T. H. White's *The Sword in the Stone*, and, well, me, I suppose. That was the plan. It seemed to me that learning about magic was the perfect story, and I was sure I could really write convincingly about school.

I wrote about five pages of the book before I realized that I had absolutely no idea what I was doing, and I stopped. (Later, I learned that most books are actually written by people who have no idea what they are doing, but go on to finish writing the books anyway. I wish I'd known that then.)

Years passed. I got married, and had children of my own, and learned how to finish writing the things I'd started.

Then one day in 1988, the telephone rang.

It was an editor in America named Karen Berger. I had recently started writing a monthly comic called *The Sandman*, which Karen was editing, although no issues had yet been published. Karen had noticed that I combined a sort of trainspotterish knowledge of minor and arcane DC Comics characters with a bizarre facility for organizing them into something more or less coherent. And also, she had an idea.

"Would you write a comic," she asked, "that would be a history of magic in the DC Comics universe, covering the past and the present and the future? Sort of a Who's Who, but with a story? We could call it *The Books of Magic*."

I said, "No, thank you." I pointed out to her how silly an idea it was—a Who's Who and a history and a travel guide that was also a story. "Quite a ridiculous idea," I said, and she apologized for having suggested it.

In bed that night I hovered at the edge of sleep, musing about Karen's call, and what a ridiculous idea it was. I mean . . . a story that would go from the beginning of time . . . to the end of time . . . and have someone meet all these strange people . . . and learn all about magic. . . .

Perhaps it wasn't so ridiculous. . . .

And then I sighed, certain that if I let myself sleep it would all be gone in the morning. I climbed out of bed and crept through the house back to my office, trying not to wake anyone in my hurry to start scribbling down ideas.

A boy. Yes. There had to be a boy. Someone smart and funny, something of an outsider, who would learn that he had the potential to be the greatest magician the world had ever seen—more powerful than Merlin. And four guides, to take him through the past, the present, through other worlds, through the future, serving the same function as the ghosts who accompany Ebenezer Scrooge through Charles Dickens's *A Christmas Carol.*

I thought for a moment about calling him Richard Grenville, after the hero of my book-I'd-never-written, but that seemed a rather too heroic name (the original Sir Richard Grenville was a sea-captain, adventurer, and explorer, after all). So I called him Tim, possibly because the Monty

Python team had shown that Tim was an unlikely sort of name for an enchanter, or with faint memories of the hero of Margaret Storey's magical children's novel, *Timothy and Two Witches*. I thought perhaps his last name should be Seekings, and it was, in the first outline I sent to Karen—a faint tribute to John Masefield's haunting tale of magic and smugglers, *The Midnight Folk*. But Karen felt this was a bit literal, so he became, in one stroke of the pen, Tim Hunter.

And as Tim Hunter he sat up, blinked, wiped his glasses on his T-shirt, and set off into the world.

(I never actually got to use the minor British Public School that taught only magic in a story, and I suppose now I never will. But I was very pleased when Mr. Croup and Mr. Vandemar finally showed up in a story about life under London, called *Neverwhere*.)

John Bolton, the first artist to draw Tim, had a son named James who was just the right age and he became John's model for Tim, tousle-haired and bespectacled. And in 1990 the first four volumes of comics that became the first *Books of Magic* graphic novel were published.

Soon enough, it seemed, Tim had a monthly series of comics chronicling his adventures and misadventures, and the slow learning process he was to undergo, as initially chronicled by author John Ney Reiber, who gave Tim a number of things—most importantly, Molly.

In this new series of novels-without-pictures, Carla Jablonski has set herself a challenging task: not only adapting Tim's stories, but also telling new ones, and through it all illuminating the saga of a young man who might just grow up to be the most powerful magician in the world. If, of course, he manages to live that long. . . .

Neil Gaiman
May 2002

Prologue

And so it shall come to pass,
A mortal child,
Like his father before him,
Shall venture into the realm.

A child at the brink of discovery
Shall arrive in the Fair Lands.
When she herself is at the brink
Her hope lies in his hands.

Need answers need.

Like his father before him,
He will have the power of transformation,
But while his father transforms in the flesh,
shedding the human at will,
The child will transform destiny.

THE FALCON'S WINGS WERE POWERFUL, and the bird shot rapidly into the sky. Tamlin, the

Queen's Falconer, shaded his brown eyes against the sun to peer up at his charge. Satisfied by its soaring circles, knowing the bird would not attempt a getaway, Tamlin's attention turned inward. He could no longer ignore the pressing questions that nagged at him.

Could it be true? he wondered. The prophecies from long ago—he had put no store in them. But now he could not keep from thinking about the possibilities. Nor could he keep his mind off the child who had come here, to this place called Faerie, and bested the Queen at one of her own games.

Tamlin had only caught a glimpse of the boy from the realm of mortals, but he had not forgotten him. A lad who could hold his own with the Queen would be remembered.

But could Timothy Hunter, who briefly visited the realm of the Fair Folk, be the child of the prophecy? If he were—and if the prophecy were true—there would be consequences for Tamlin, the Queen, even for Timothy himself. Because of this, Tamlin did not know even his own heart— what to hope or whether hope was possible. Tamlin did not want to be deceived again. He had been deceived too easily in the past by the glamours of Faerie.

The falconer sighed. There were too many

times he had allowed himself to be deceived by this land. Faerie had offered untold pleasures: beauty, joy, and delight. A caressing breeze, sparkling brooks, beckoning lakes, wild forests dappled and mysterious. But that was before everything changed. *One believes what one wants to*, Tamlin mused, *and Faerie herself seems to encourage self-delusion, finding secret ways to make it easier to accept what should be unacceptable. She has the power to conjure illusion and create delusion.* Tamlin's long tenure in this world had made that painfully apparent.

Tamlin raised his gloved hand to signal the falcon he was training. *And what of the Queen?* Tamlin wondered. *She is so practiced at pretense it would be hard to glean what she knows of Faerie, of the prophecy, of anything.* The majestic bird swooped down and landed neatly on Tamlin's wrist. Its talons gripped the thick leather of his glove. Tamlin spoke soothingly to the bird as it preened, then lowered a hood over the bird's head. "You and I are the same," he told the bird. "We soar to our heart's content, but we have only the illusion of freedom."

Tamlin scanned the horizon. It pained him to see what had become of the royal hunting grounds. Where once majestic trees had sheltered myriad animals, now there stood withered, gnarled deformities. Beyond them were the devastated valleys, the choked and thirsty ground cracked and dead. Like all of Faerie.

He knew he must act, and soon.

Titania, Queen of Faerie, stood at the low marble wall that surrounded a patio behind the palace. The twilight sky matched her mood as it transformed the pale and placid scene into something darker and more intense.

That child, she thought, *that child who arrived from the realm of the mortals. And yet—his power.* It simply made no sense to her. Unless . . .

Have I been deceived? she wondered, her golden eyes narrowing. She did not see the scene before her, the courtiers strolling the paths, sprites making sport on the crystalline lake, the pretty flitlings hovering nearby awaiting her command. What she saw was treachery, duplicity, and danger. She, too, was distracted by the ancient prophecies. All those years ago— What had *truly* happened to the child? She thought he had died, had been told of it, but had not witnessed it herself. She should not have been so foolish; but she had placed more stock in trust then, and some would say trust is cherished by fools. Today it would have been different, and she would not be facing this . . . this astonishing possibility.

This could be a boon, she realized. Anger over the possibility that the child of the prophecy was still alive, over being lied to, should not cloud her recognition of the advantage the child could pose. But at the same time, the prophecy might not be true at all. And the child, despite her suspicions, may still very well be gone.

Trust. Despite her hesitation, trust was what she had to count on, and it was such a tricky thing. Tamlin had never lied to her, more's the pity. There were certainly times when she wished that he had. In the past, he'd hidden things from her but when asked a direct question he inevitably gave her a direct answer, even if that answer put him in danger of her wrath.

Yes. He was the only one she could ask, the only one who could find out the truth. But how would he react to this news? *He may have already solved this riddle*, she realized. In which case, she wanted to be included in whatever knowledge he had.

She shut her eyes and felt the breeze growing cooler as the sun fell below the horizon.

"Come, my Falconer." She summoned Tamlin with her mind by picturing him. She heard a flutter of wings and smiled.

"Why have you called me?" a growling voice demanded.

Titania slowly opened her eyes. Tamlin—tall, lean, muscular; the betrayed and betrayer; her beloved and despised one—stood before her. His straight brown hair hung to his shoulders, framing his angular face. Adversary and only true friend. They had so much history between them it hung thick and heavy in the air whenever they were together.

Now that he was here, she was unsure how to proceed. With everyone else—even with her husband King Auberon—she did as she would without a thought, not a twinge of concern about what she might be asking or doing. Yet with Tamlin she was humbled. She wanted his approval, particularly because he rarely gave it.

She didn't look at him; instead, she kept her eyes fixed in front of her. She noticed a few of the tiny flitlings buzzing nearby and waved them away. Gossip would not be welcome. She nodded at the two armed servants who had placed themselves discreetly just beyond earshot. There were always several bodyguards around. It would attract too much attention if she dismissed them—it would be too obvious that this was a personal matter.

"I have been wondering . . . about that boy," she said. She kept her voice light, as if this were nothing but idle curiosity.

"What boy?" Tamlin asked.

This time she looked at him, an eyebrow raised. She was letting him know that she was aware he knew precisely what boy she was talking about.

"Ah." Tamlin said. "The mortal one, who made his way into this world not long ago."

"Yes, him." She sat on the wall, her back to the lawn. She spotted her jester, Amadan, peering down at them from her bedchamber window in the turret. What was he doing up there? Spying, she assumed. She made sure Amadan knew that she saw him. She might need him, but she wanted him to remember who was in charge. That flitling was small, but he held most of the court in his thrall, always scheming, stirring up intrigues within intrigues.

She smoothed her long skirt over her knees. The light breeze made the translucent pastel chiffon layers flutter. "I am glad he was brought to me."

Tamlin nodded, waiting for her to play her hand.

"I sense great power in Timothy Hunter," Titania said. "He bears watching. I want you to bring him back here. Now."

Tamlin's brown eyes were opaque; she could not tell what he was thinking.

"Did you hear me?" she demanded, growing

impatient. She tossed her long locks over her shoulder. "I want you to fetch him. Bring him here to me."

"No. I will not." Tamlin stated firmly. Then, as if it were the most natural thing in the world, he transformed into a falcon and soared away.

Chapter One

I ALWAYS KNEW THAT GYM CLASS WAS
state-supported torture, Timothy Hunter thought.
After all, forcing us to play football outdoors in this
weather is clearly cruel and unusual punishment.

Tim hovered on the outskirts of the game.
Sports—other than skateboarding—were not his
strong suit. He felt foolish in his gym outfit.
Gooseflesh covered his skin, and his baggy shirt
only emphasized his lack of muscles. His father
said Tim was undergoing a growth spurt and that
it was typical at thirteen years old to do so. But it
made his arms and legs gangly; and his skinny
wrists and ankles were always poking out of
sleeves and cuffs.

To make matters worse, Molly O'Reilly's
class was running laps around the perimeter of
the playing field. The last thing Tim wanted was
for her to see him miss a pass or trip over his own

shoelaces. Not that she was impressed by sports types, but he still didn't want to look like a dolt. So he tried to make himself as inconspicuous as possible. He didn't want anything he did to be interpreted as an invitation to his teammates to send the ball his way. As he hung back, away from the others, he realized he might be more conspicuous on his own.

Uh-oh. He was right. Molly saluted to him as she jogged by. Her curly brown hair was pulled back into a ponytail that bounced in rhythm with her feet. She was fast, he noticed, and she wasn't even breaking a sweat.

He didn't want to insult her by not waving back. He pushed his glasses up to the bridge of his nose and then lifted his arm. He held it close to his side and only moved his hand back and forth. Sort of how the Royals waved as they drove by in a parade. He used as little movement as possible so as not to attract the attention of his teammates. He glanced over at Bobby Saunders, who had the ball. *Safe*, Tim thought. *Bobby never passes to anyone.*

Tim went back to daydreaming. His mind was so full these days—how could anyone expect him to concentrate on something as ordinary as a silly football match? So much had happened to him, and he was still trying to understand it.

Not too long ago, Timothy had been pretty much like any other thirteen-year-old boy in a London council home. Then four strangers arrived and informed him that he had the potential to become the most powerful magician the world had ever seen. Heavy stuff. Needless to say, things changed pretty radically after that.

These men—the Trenchcoat Brigade, as he called them—took him to other worlds. The one known only as the Stranger brought him into the past. Tim witnessed the sinking of Atlantis, saw ancient civilizations, and even met Merlin. Then John Constantine took him to America and introduced him to other magic types of the present day. Tim's favorite part of the trip was meeting Zatanna, a lady magician he had admired on TV. She turned out to be even cooler in person. Next, it was on to Faerie, a magical realm that seemed straight out of a storybook.

Faerie had been amazing. It wasn't just that it was probably the prettiest, most spectacular place he'd ever seen. It was where he felt like magic was real. More than that—that magic was natural, everyday, and ordinary but in an extraordinary way. He had met talking animals, nasty little creatures, and beautiful fairies who could fly and sing, and even the air there made him want to dance—if he were keen on dancing.

He almost wound up a prisoner there, when the Queen, Titania, tricked him into accepting a gift. But he managed to find a way out and was able to return home. Then, of course, no adventure would be complete without an attempt on one's life. And Tim had been there, done that, too. His creepy tour guide, Mr. E, took him into the future, to the "end of time," and then turned on him and tried to drive a stake through his heart. It was a bizarre miracle that Tim had made it back alive.

Throughout all the journeys, it seemed like there were always people trying to kill him or take his magic. John Constantine, the bloke Tim liked best of the crew, had explained that Tim's magic could go either way—good or evil—and that there were powerful forces who wanted to be sure his magic went the way they wanted it to—or didn't go at all. In other words, if Tim wasn't going to work for the bad guys, they wanted him dead!

Am I still in danger? Tim wondered. Since the Trenchcoat Brigade had deposited him at home that rainy night a little over a month ago, exhausted and confused, nothing unusual had happened. In a strange way it was a little disappointing. *Now what? What do I do with this information?*

Even though Tim had spent the whole time scared stiff, it was the most alive he had ever felt.

Maybe because so many times I thought I was about to be dead, he reasoned.

Tim thought about things he'd seen and magic he'd *done*. When they first met, Dr. Occult, the one who had shown Tim the land of Faerie, had turned Tim's yo-yo into an owl. At the end of time, when Mr. E had attacked him, Yo-yo flew in front of the stake that had been intended for Tim. Yo-yo's sacrifice had saved Tim, but killed the owl. Back at home after the Trenchcoat Brigade had left him, after Tim had rejected magic, frustrated and disappointed and alone, Tim had managed to somehow turn his yo-yo back into a bird. *How did I do that?* he wondered.

But the bird had flown away. And Tim missed him.

A movement overhead caught Tim's eye. He squinted up and saw a large bird circling above him. "Yo-yo?"

Just then he felt a thud against his ankle and glanced down. The football sat beside his foot. "Oh," Tim said. "I suppose I should do something with that."

"Yikes!" he cried, as the opposing team thundered toward him. *Oh no!* His teammates were heading straight toward him, too!

Tim tried to kick the ball away, but it had now rolled out of reach.

Ooof! The large boy who sat three rows in front of him in Literature class slammed into Tim. Tim landed on the ground, winded, his face grinding into the dirt, as three more kids piled on top of him. Then he heard a shout. "Saunders has the ball!" Everyone scrambled away, leaving Tim sore and humiliated, alone on the grass.

Slowly, Tim sat up. He felt around and found his glasses. Luckily, they weren't broken. Tim's ribs twinged where someone's knees had connected with them. He felt trampled. He stood up and felt worse. He saw that Molly had stopped running and witnessed the entire fiasco.

"Brilliant," he muttered, "just brilliant." He started to jog. He planned to run toward the others, to prove he wasn't a complete wimp and weakling. But instead, he bypassed the knot of players in the scrimmage and kept going. He picked up speed and tore out of the schoolyard.

"Hunter!" he heard his gym teacher, Coach Michelson, shout behind him. "Hunter! Where do you think you're going?"

Tim ignored him, ignored everything. It was all just a blur as his feet pounded the pavement.

What is wrong with me? Tim admonished himself. *I am such a loser. How can I possibly be this powerful magician that the entire universe is after, when I can't hold my own on the bloody schoolyard?*

No wonder Yo-yo abandoned me.

Footfall after footfall, the running jangled his bruised body, but it felt good, as if he were landing punches on an unseen adversary—and that enemy was his own confusion. He felt like he would explode out of his skin.

This change, this magic event, this was big. Too big for him to sit still, too big to play stupid football, too big to explain to anyone. Even to Molly.

His breaths were ragged now. He couldn't slow down, couldn't stop running. His chest hurt, but he didn't stop. The pain was *real*—it made sense. It wasn't like that magic stuff. Run hard, breathe hard. Logic. His thoughts were now taking on the rhythm of his feet. Fairy Queens? Magic keys? Past worlds? Tim stopped and grabbed a lamppost, bending over and panting. *How can that have happened to me? How could it have happened to anyone?*

He slid down and sat on the pavement, leaning against the lamppost, sweat pouring down his face. He knew he'd feel chilled soon, sweating in the cold December air, but he didn't care.

No one would believe me. Not even Molly. And I don't want her to think I've gone completely mad. I need her to be my friend. And she wouldn't be friends with a raving loon. Well, he thought getting to his feet, *she probably would. She wouldn't drop someone*

just because he deserved to be committed, not Molly.
But Tim didn't want a friend who cared for him
only because she felt sorry for him. He did want
someone to confide in, but how could he tell
anyone about an experience for which he couldn't
find the words?

Tim glanced around to get his bearings, then
laughed. He'd run all the way home. He'd gone
the long way, past the boarded-up shops and
behind the parking garage. He had added about
fifteen blocks to the route, but now his home in
Ravenknoll Estates was just a few streets over.
He might as well go there.

If he told her, Molly might think it was all just
a dream, Tim thought as he slowly walked up to
his front door. He had trouble believing it was not
a dream himself. He had met Merlin, back in the
time of King Arthur. He had traveled to America
with John Constantine in no time at all, literally.
Of *course* it sounded like a dream.

Then he paused. *Only it wasn't a dream.*

Tim slogged up to the door, then realized his
keys were in his jacket in his locker back at
school.

Great. He wouldn't be able to sneak in, hoping
his distracted, depressed father wouldn't notice.
He'd have to knock and explain himself. Well,
today already stunk. Why not let it stink worse?

He knocked. He heard the television blaring from the living room, then noticed the curtain in the front window move.

His father opened the door. "Tim?"

Father and son looked at each other. Tim saw his dad's fleshy face, his thinning hair, the paunch his cardigan stretched over, the missing button. Tim wondered what his dad saw looking at him. Tim figured he himself looked a wreck; he certainly *felt* a wreck.

Uh-oh. On further observation Tim recognized that his dad was 100% alert today, for once. The clues were small but there.

The car accident that had taken Tim's mother's life had also caused Tim's father to lose an arm. Today the empty sleeve of his father's gray sweater was neatly pinned up. Some days— the bad ones—Mr. Hunter let the empty sleeve dangle, if he got dressed at all. On those days he paid far less attention to Tim, shouting out only for him to come watch some old black-and-white movie on television or to ask absentmindedly how school was, even on a Saturday. Those days, Tim could get away with anything.

"Have you lost your key again? I swear, lad, you'd lose your head if it weren't attached to your shoulders."

Tim pushed past him and entered the house.

His father shifted in the doorway and peered at him.

"Tim, what are you doing home at this hour? And where are your school clothes?" His father began to follow him. "What happened to you, lad? Did you get into a fight?"

Tim didn't answer, just trudged up the stairs to his room, shut the door, and lay facedown on his bed.

Every muscle hurt. He'd been quite trampled. How was that considered education?

The downstairs phone rang, and Tim heard his father answer. *Good.* That meant he'd leave Tim alone a little while longer.

"Yes?" Mr. Hunter said. There was a long pause, and then his voice had an edge to it. "Is that a fact? I shouldn't take that tone if I were you. If anyone wants sorting out for negligence it's your gym instructor."

Did I think the phone call was a good thing? Now I'm going to catch it for sure. Tim stood and crossed to his door. He opened it a crack so he could hear his father's side of the conversation better. It wasn't hard, since his father was getting louder as he got angrier.

"Oh no?" Mr. Hunter said. "What do you call it when my boy limps in with a split lip? He's putting up a brave front, but I think he's got a cracked rib or two. As a matter of fact, I was about to run him in for an X ray."

Tim's forehead furrowed. His father was defending him to the school?

"Fine," Mr. Hunter snapped. "Just so we're clear on one thing. My Tim is not an incorrigible anything. Good-bye."

Tim heard his father slam the phone down. Then he heard the creaking of the stairs. He quickly grabbed a book from his desk, sat on his bed, and flipped the book open, trying to not look incorrigible.

"Hullo?" Mr. Hunter hovered in the doorway, then stepped into Tim's room. He seemed ill at ease. Uncertain.

Tim didn't know what was coming, so he didn't know what to do. "Hullo," he replied.

"Well, I just thought I'd . . ." Mr. Hunter glanced around Tim's room, surprised. "What's all this? No skateboarding chaps on the wall? Owls, is it now?"

"I like owls. Doesn't everyone?"

Mr. Hunter perched on the edge of Tim's bed. "Errrr. Beautiful day outside, isn't it?"

This is a brilliant conversation, Tim thought. "Yeah. Looks sort of like yesterday. Quite a lot like yesterday, actually."

"What I mean is, nice as it is, why don't you go outside and play?"

"Play?" Tim stared at his dad. He sensed worry and concern—two emotions his father rarely displayed. Self-absorbed melancholy was more his dad's style.

"You've been looking a bit peaked, lately."

"Peaked?" *Who is this man*, Tim wondered, *and what have they done with my father?*

"Really, Tim, you're getting to be a regular recluse. Don't think I haven't noticed." *Dad has noticed me? This* is *news.* In addition to surprise, Tim also felt it was too little, too late. "But—"

"No buts about it," his dad said, getting up. "You get dressed and get out there and have some fun. Skate or play ball or something."

"All right. I'll go outside and frolic, then," Tim said. "I'll get dressed on my own, though. If you don't mind. I can do that, you know. I can tie my own shoelaces and everything."

"Tim." Mr. Hunter sighed and left the room. Tim changed into a pair of jeans and a long-sleeved shirt. He threw a sweatshirt over his head, grabbed his jacket, and left the house.

"Why don't you go outside and play?" he muttered, repeating his father's inane recommendation. As if a round of catch was going to solve his problems.

Does he think I'm a little kid? When a bit of fresh

air might have been all that was needed to change my point of view?

Tim kicked an empty soda can into the gutter. *He calls me a recluse? Look who's talking! I suppose when one sits in front of the telly all day, one has time to notice these things. Besides,* Tim thought, bending down and grabbing a broken tree branch, *Dad should be pleased about my solitary existence.* Tim dragged the branch along the broken-down mesh fence surrounding an empty lot. *Chip off the old block and all that.*

He tossed the stick aside. *Maybe I* should *go talk to Molly. Feel her out.* It was possible that if Tim explained it all very carefully Molly wouldn't think he was a complete and utter loon. He knew he'd feel better if he had someone he could tell. *Molly's the best of the best when it comes to keeping secrets.* Still . . .

He had arrived at the edge of the park and still couldn't decide.

"Man-child," Tim heard behind him. He turned to see a stocky man wearing a long dark overcoat and a hat with a wide brim pulled low over his face. He had a broad, sagging face with eyes that seemed too far apart. The man grinned, and Tim saw he was missing several teeth. Tim immediately had a "Trenchcoat Brigade" flashback and wondered if the whole thing was starting over again. Then the strange man pointed to the sky. "Look up."

Curious, Tim looked up. A large bird circled above him—like the one he had seen at school. Then it quickly fluttered away, vanishing behind a building. "Yo-yo?" Tim murmured.

Someone standing behind him said, "No, not Yo-yo."

Tim jerked sharply to one side and took off running. He suddenly knew for certain that the person behind him was going to try to grab him and that the thick man in front of him must have been the diversion. *No way!*

Tim twisted and swerved and ran into the park. He quickly arrived at a thickly wooded section, leaping over heavy roots and ducking under bare branches. There were dead leaves on the ground, and Tim could hear the crunching of his pursuers' feet behind him.

He put on speed. In fact, he pumped his feet so fast he never saw the net that was stretched between two bushes before it had snagged him.

"Oof!" he cried out as he tripped and stumbled, caught in his midsection by the net. He saw that two burly men in identical hats and overcoats were gripping the edges of the strong net. When he was just inches from landing facedown on the ground, a powerful hand jerked Tim's head back by his hair and held him upright. Tim gulped. He felt the cold blade of a knife at his throat.

"Keep your voice to a whisper if you know what's good for you," a deep voice said.

No problem, Tim thought. He was too afraid to speak.

The men holding the net seemed surprised to see the man who was holding his knife to Tim. "What are you doing here?" one of them asked.

What's going on? Aren't these goons working together? Tim tried hard not to move. Any wriggle made the man's grip on his hair tighter, and he really didn't want that knife blade to press any harder against his skin.

"Are you here to help?" the other man holding the net asked. He seemed peeved. "Did she think we couldn't do this on our own?"

The man gripping Tim ignored the other two men. He concentrated on Tim. "I will release you if you give me your word that you will not run away."

"All right," Tim choked out. "I promise."

"Swear by your name," the man demanded.

Now that's another thing entirely, Tim thought. *I'm not giving up my name to this bloke. I learn from my mistakes.* "No," Tim replied. He cringed a little, waiting for the man's reaction.

A begrudging smile crossed the man's lean face. "Very well. You know the value of names, I see."

The man lowered the knife but kept a powerful grip on Tim's shoulder. Unrelenting, he quickly bound Tim's wrists together with thin leather straps. Then he lowered a hood over Tim's head. Tim felt the man hoist him up onto his shoulders as if he were no more than an overloaded knapsack.

"Hey!" Tim protested, but the sound was muffled by the hood.

"You two go home," Tim heard his kidnapper tell the others.

"She will be furious if we return without him," one of the men protested.

"She's not here. I am," the man said. "And now I'm not!"

With that statement, the world seemed to vanish. Tim felt a rush of air as his abductor transported them away to somewhere.

Tim had felt this rush before—on his journey through time and space. It could only mean one thing; his abductor was magic!

Chapter Two

TIM FELT A POUNDING HEAT. The hood he wore grew stifling, and his shirt clung to his sweating skin. He felt none of the woozy nausea he had experienced the first time he'd been magicked across planes of reality.

I suppose I'm getting used to it, Tim thought, *becoming an old hand at this magical travel. Maybe I should look into becoming an astral guide—cruise director for magical journeys.*

He felt himself being lowered to the ground.

"Hold still," Tim was ordered.

Tim obeyed—what else could he do? The hood covering his head was removed roughly.

"Oy!" Tim cried. The hood had dragged his glasses off his face, scraping his skin. He blinked against the punishing sun, then scanned the rocky ground for his specs. He hated feeling as helpless as he did without them.

A large, gloved hand appeared under Tim's nose. It held his glasses. Tim squinted up at his abductor.

Tim wasn't sure whether or not the man was offering the glasses to him.

"What's wrong with your eyes?" the man asked.

"What's it to you?" Tim snapped.

The man moved his hand out of reach. Clearly he wasn't going to give Tim his glasses until he got an answer.

"Okay," Tim grumbled. "I'm nearsighted."

The man turned the glasses over and then peered through them. "Ah. You need these to see what's in the distance?"

This bloke has never seen eyeglasses before? Where's he been? "Yes. Can I have them back, please?"

The man nodded and held them out to Tim, who grabbed the glasses awkwardly, his wrists still bound together. He put them on and took a better look at the stranger.

The man was tall, and he had a weathered face that bore the unmistakable signs of outdoor life. His long straight hair was lighter than Tim's, but his eyes were the same shade of brown. He wore a long leather coat, high leather boots, and one glove. His shirt and trousers were of some soft material Tim had never seen, and they were the purplish color of twilight. A large, smooth stone hung around his neck on a leather cord.

He settled onto a boulder and seemed to be studying Tim as intently as Tim was studying him. Tim wondered how he was measuring up. This scrutiny was worse than being kidnapped. Tim felt as if he were being tested, and he didn't even know in what subject.

The man leaned forward and held up the curved hunting knife that not too long ago had been pressed against Tim's throat. "Hold out your hands," he said.

Tim hesitated. That knife looked awfully sharp.

The man's brown eyes never wavered from Tim's, and he held very still, as if a sudden movement might cause Tim to bolt. The man nodded once as if to say "it's all right, chap," and gestured with his gloved hand for Tim to come closer.

Tim held out his arms and the man cut the bindings. Tim rubbed his sore wrists. Those leather ties were tight!

The man tossed his knife to the dirt, stood, and paced. Now that Tim felt less vulnerable, and his kidnapper was farther away and unarmed, he was able to take in his surroundings. They seemed to be in some vast desert. There was nothing green anywhere. It was all dirt, tumbleweed, boulders, and rocks under a bleached-out sky. Tim and this man were probably the only living things for miles; nothing could survive in this bleak landscape.

Finally the man addressed Tim. "You may ask me three questions. That's the rule."

Tim raised an eyebrow. So wherever they were, there were rules and this man was abiding by them. That gave Tim a bit of courage, even though he didn't know what any of those rules might be.

"What do you want with me?" There. Tim had asked his first question. Straight and to the point.

"I want to find out what you're made of," the man responded.

Hm. Does he mean literally? As in, flesh, blood, and bone? Or like in the nursery rhyme—snips and snails and puppy dog tails. It occurred to Tim that might be what the knife was for—to dissect him like a frog in biology class. Then Tim decided that, despite all the weirdness he'd been through, his imagination was working overtime. This guy wouldn't have gone to all the trouble of kidnapping Tim and bringing him to this place as a lab experiment. No. He must mean something else. Which was just as confusing.

"Why?" Tim asked. *What does it matter to this*

bloke what sort of person I am?

"Look around you, boy," the man ordered. "You're no stranger to this twilight realm, I know. So tell me. Have you ever seen such pretty groves or heard a river make such music anywhere but in Faerie?"

The man knelt down in a shallow trench, and Tim realized it had once been a riverbed—a river that had gone dry ages ago, judging by the looks of things.

"This is Faerie? I don't believe you," Tim scoffed. "I've been to Faerie, and it's all green and pretty and full of flowers."

The man smiled sadly. "It has been that. It is not that now. Not here where we can truly see."

"You haven't answered my question," Tim pointed out.

"Haven't I?" The man gave him a quizzical look.

"I asked you why you wanted to find out what I'm made of."

The man turned his back to Tim and gazed out across the wasteland. He sounded weary. "Because this land was once alive and I would have it live again." He turned to face Tim. "And you may or may not be the key to the healing of it."

Whoa. That wasn't the answer Tim had expected. And this bloke certainly hadn't been treating him like the answer to all of his problems. "So you kidnap and threaten me? Of course, it all makes perfect sense," Tim said sarcastically.

Everyone is acting like their opposites today, Tim thought. *First, Dad plays devoted parent, and now this one treats me worse than an enemy, when what he wants is my help.*

The man kept his back to Tim. His knife still lay on the ground between them. Tim had a feeling he was being tested.

"It's no use trying to make me mad," Tim said. "I'm not going to grab your stupid knife."

The man spun around, his face cruel. "Do you want to die here?" he growled.

Tim lunged forward to grab the knife. As he did, his toe nicked a pebble, and he stumbled, catching his foot on his ankle. He went sprawling to the ground. Furious, frustrated, and humiliated, he scrambled for the knife, although the man was standing still, just observing.

Tim picked up the knife, scowled at it, then flung it aside. "I don't like tests," he grumbled. He sat cross-legged on the ground. "I always mess up." *Particularly the grab-a-weapon-while-you-can kind of test.*

The man picked up his knife. "If you're going to ask a third question, you'd best ask now. It's time."

Tim knew exactly the question he wanted to ask. It was what he'd learned was important during his first visit to Faerie. "What is your name?"

Tim waited for the man's reaction. He might get mad—it was considered impolite to ask a person his name. Instead, you were supposed to ask someone, "What are you called?" That was because names had power, Tim had discovered, and knowing someone's true name meant you had power over him. It told you a truth about him.

It had taken Tim a bit of time to learn that lesson. But his guides, the Trenchcoat Brigade, had given his name to several people on their journey, which in retrospect was a little disturbing. It suddenly occurred to him: *Maybe "Timothy Hunter" isn't my "true" name. Maybe "Timothy Hunter" is simply what I am called.*

Tim decided to think about the implications of that little idea later.

The man seemed to consider the question, then said, "Tamlin."

Tim's eyes never left the man's rugged face. *Is that his true name?* Tim wondered.

"So you have my name," Tamlin said. "Will you curse me now?"

Interesting. It is *his real name.*

"Curse me all you want," Tamlin said, almost

as if he were daring Tim to do so. "You wouldn't be the first. Nor, I imagine, will you be the last. That has been my road."

Go all pathetic, why don't you? Tim thought. The man's complaints didn't match his rugged appearance. "Do you feel sorry for yourself all the time? Or just when you're terrorizing people?"

Tamlin gave Tim a sharp look and took a step closer to him. "If a man said that to me, I'd feed him slices of his heart until he choked."

"I'm sure you would," Tim scoffed. He rolled his eyes dramatically.

Tim's head snapped back as the man cracked his hand across his face.

"You need to learn respect, child," Tamlin said.

Tim blinked his eyes. He was more startled than hurt, but he wasn't going to give this creep the satisfaction of seeing him react. He made his face go blank.

"You're fearless enough, I'll give you that," Tamlin said. Tim could hear approval in his voice. "And you have vision. Vision enough to know that some truths are best unspoken." Tamlin laughed. "Keep your insights to yourself, boy. Not everyone appreciates your sort of wisdom. If you learn nothing else from me, learn that."

Tim said nothing; he glared at Tamlin. He

didn't trust his voice to speak.

Tamlin yanked the amulet he wore around his neck so hard the leather cord snapped. He held it up, and the stone glinted in the bright light. Tim could not place the color. One minute, it seemed to be purplish blue. At another angle it glowed silver. From another it looked deep red.

"You've done well, Timothy Hunter," Tamlin said, "very well. I had not thought you would."

"Well, I like that!" Tim protested. "You assumed I'd fail your stupid test?" He didn't bother to ask how Tamlin knew what to call him. Magical people all seemed well aware that he was called "Timothy Hunter," as if it were posted on a bulletin board somewhere.

Tamlin ignored Tim's outburst. He held out the amulet. "This is yours now. Take it."

"No way," Tim declared. "If this really is Faerie, then I know the rules. If I take a gift from you I have to reciprocate in a manner you choose. I'm never fooled the same way twice."

Tamlin grinned. "You do learn your lessons, don't you? Well, let me assure you, this is no Faerie trick. You see, I am not one of the Fair Folk. You and I can exchange gifts without repercussion."

Tim's eyes narrowed as he tried to determine if Tamlin was telling the truth.

"You have my name," Tamlin reminded him. "I swear by it that I give this to you with no expectation or price."

"Okay, then."

Tamlin handed Tim the amulet. It was a heavy stone, cool despite the sun beating down on it. Now it was a golden-bronze color. "What is it?" Tim asked.

"In your hands? I can't say. It could be I've dared my Queen's anger, and much more, to give you nothing. Some things are what you make of them."

Tim sighed. *Why does everyone in these strange places speak in riddles?*

"It has been called an Opening Stone," Tamlin added. "What it opens will be up to you."

Tim gazed down at the Opening Stone. When he glanced back, Tamlin was a small figure in the distance. How did he get away so quickly? And why would he just split like that?

Tim scrambled to his feet. "Hey! Hey wait!" he called. "Where are you going?"

Tamlin got smaller and smaller. Tim began to run. What would he do if Tamlin left him here in the desert?

"Wait! Come back! How am I supposed to get home?"

Tamlin disappeared behind a rock. Tim put on

a burst of speed and rounded the large boulder.

"You can't just leave . . ." Tamlin was nowhere in sight. All that remained were his long coat, his boots, his shirt, and his trousers. Tim's eyes widened. *The guy is out wandering around—naked?* Tim noticed he had also left behind his knife and his gauntlet. *Weird.* But no matter how hard Tim peered into the distance, no matter which direction he looked, he saw nothing but empty landscape. The only sign of life was a large hawk circling overheard.

Great, Tim thought. *Alone in a desert with a bird.*

Chapter Three

TIM SANK ONTO THE BOULDER AND kicked a pebble. "Gone. He's just gone," he muttered.

I don't get it. I passed his stupid test. So why would he leave me out here to fry? Oh. Because this is a test, too, Tim realized, *a big one: to get myself home.*

As much as Tim hated to admit it, even to himself, he wanted to do well on this test. He wanted that Tamlin bloke's respect. *Besides, it is bloody hot in the desert, and as bad as gym class and Ravenknoll Estates may be, I don't want to die here. After all I've been through recently, that would be a dumb way to sign out.*

Tim tried to remember details from adventure films about surviving in the desert. *First thing, cover your head. Don't want to go all heat stroke-ish.* He removed his sweatshirt and wrapped it around his head in a kind of turban.

He looked at the clothing Tamlin had left

behind. "So he's abandoned you, too," Tim said to the leather coat.

That has got to be expensive, Tim thought. He lifted up the coat. _Oof._ It weighed a ton. _Forget about bringing it to Bertram's Used Clothes Emporium to fetch some pocket money_. No way was Tim going to lug that hefty item around in the desert.

The boots were far too big for him—no use there. He stared at the gauntlet and the knife. He shook his head. "Another bloody test." He decided to leave them behind. He had no need for hand-me-downs.

He gripped the amulet that Tamlin had given him. "Which way?" he murmured, studying the landscape. The stone grew warm in his hand. Startled, Tim wondered if the rise in temperature was due to his own body heat warming it or if it had responded to his question.

Tim looked at Tamlin's large footprints in the sand, which ended at the pile of clothes. He figured his way back home was not going to be in the same direction Tamlin had taken. Tim stepped into the deep impressions, facing the opposite way.

Tim shut his eyes and concentrated on the stone. It was smoother and rounder on one end than the other, like an arrowhead, only it wasn't flat. Would it answer his question?

"Which way?" he asked. This time he said it loudly, as if he were demanding an answer.

The stone grew warm again. Tim took a step. Then he turned right and took several more steps. Now the stone's temperature dropped. He hastily returned to his original spot. Once again, the stone grew warm.

"Like that kids' game," Tim realized. "Getting warmer, getting colder." Holding the stone out in front of him like a compass, Tim began making his way through the desert.

Nothing about his surroundings reminded him in the slightest of Faerie. The land he had visited was lively and beautiful, filled with lakes, trees, valleys, and creatures of all variety. There were smells and sounds and crisp, clean air. Here was . . . nothing. Grit. Dust. Silence. The only sounds were Tim's raspy breathing and the crunching noise his feet made on the pebbles underfoot. The only smells were his own sweat and gravel, and the air felt heavy.

Tim trudged on. He was getting thirsty. There were several problems with that. First, there didn't seem to be any water around. Second, if this strange, sad place *was* Faerie, then he couldn't eat or drink anything here anyway or he would be trapped forever. It was one of the rules of the place. But he didn't know how much longer he could last. The sun was starting to set, so at least it would cool down. But the wind was picking up. The breeze chilled the sweat coating his body.

Tim had to stop. He sank to his knees. He was starting to shiver with hunger, fatigue, and maybe even fear. He held the stone. *I wish I was home*, he thought. *Now.*

And he was.

Chapter Four

TAMLIN KNELT DOWN AND SCOOPED UP a handful of red sand, allowing it to sift through his fingers. He picked up a dead tree branch and placed it in the small leather sack he had retrieved after returning to human form. The twigs were signs of withering. *Evidence my lady would deny*, Tamlin thought, *as she denies all she finds disturbing*.

Still crouching, he scooped up another handful and this time filled his sack with the sand. *What's out of sight is out of mind for my lady*, he mused. *She sees only what pleases her. She has such an ability for this that she still sees Faerie as a lush paradise—filled with natural wonders. She literally can't see the dust—she can't see what Faerie has become.* Tamlin shook his head. He wished sometimes that he could do the same.

"Falconer!" A voice called out behind him.

Tamlin slowly turned his head but didn't bother getting up. "Mazaran," Tamlin greeted the Queen's courtier. "I didn't know you spoke to mortals."

"My Queen requires your presence, Falconer. I believe she is angry with you."

"Is she? She'll be angrier soon."

"Spare me your insolence. Move. Now."

"Wait." Tamlin felt the sharp edge of Mazaran's blade on the back of his neck.

"Wait for what?" Mazaran demanded.

"For the wind to shift." Tamlin scooped up more sand. "There!" He tossed the sand into Mazaran's face.

"Aggh!" the courtier cried. His hands flew to his face, and he stumbled first to his knees and then to the ground.

"Dog's son," Mazaran cursed. "You've blinded me."

"So I see," Tamlin replied. "But it's only sand, Mazaran. Cry for a while and when you're done, you'll be no blinder than you've been all your life."

Tamlin turned his back on the Faerie courtier. "Pity the elf lord," Tamlin called out to the empty landscape, "vanquished by dirt."

Tamlin threw his head back and held out his arms. His body shimmered and shrunk: arms into wings, feet into talons. Feathers sprouted where once there was only skin. Tamlin discarded his human shape as easily as his clothing—once again transforming into a falcon.

His wings pumped, taking him higher and higher into the sky while the courtier still lay sniveling on the ground. The freedom of flight was exhilarating and Tamlin never tired of it.

Mazaran is like all the rest of his Faerie kindred, Tamlin thought as he soared toward the Queen's castle. *Arrogant. Contemptuous of mortal kind. And like all the rest of them, prone to overlooking the obvious. Until some scapegrace like me throws it in his face.*

Tamlin saw the turrets of the castle beyond the next rise. In Tamlin's eyes the rolling hills had lost their green luster, but he knew that most of Faerie's inhabitants—perhaps all—saw only lush green carpets of grass and flowers. Tamlin saw the truth, while the Fair Folk saw an illusion.

It is the way of the Fair Folk to veil the real with enchantment, Tamlin thought. *They cloak all that is drab or dull or flawed with spells of glamour—and so now they cloak the reality of what Faerie has become in the same way.*

Tamlin knew that to the Fair Folk, as something was, it always would be. Nothing ever changed. The ability to see reality and to change was man's magic. *My magic*, Tamlin thought. He was aware that one day this trait could be the death of him. Perhaps that day would be today.

Am I giving you what you want, Titania? he wondered. *Will my truth provide you with an excuse to cut off my head for treason? No matter. I do what I must.*

Ah, Titania. Tamlin circled the palace grounds searching for the Queen, the twig he had retrieved earlier in his beak. *I wish there were a gentler way to shake the sleep from your eyes. I warned you that the borderlands were crumbling, but you laughed and dismissed me. The decay has worsened, milady. And I can't be gentle any longer.*

He spotted Titania below, asleep on one of the settees on the back terrace. He would wake her now. Once and for all.

Titania's long hair spread out on an embroidered pillow, her elegant gown draped fetchingly. Tamlin landed and worked the change that transformed him back into a man. He removed the branch from his mouth and held it in his hand. "Wake up, Titania," he said. "I've brought you a gift. Something you're not often given. Truth."

Titania's ever-changing eyes fluttered open. They were a deep violet now, still heavy with sleep. "You're raving, Falconer," she murmured. "I find it tedious."

With a demure yawn, she sat up and leaned against the cushions. "What is this present you said you brought me?"

"Truth," Tamlin declared, "a truth even you should find difficult to ignore."

Titania raised a disapproving eyebrow. "You have worn a bird's shape for too long, Falconer," she scolded. "You've forgotten gentle speech, it seems. And clear speech as well." She gave an impatient shrug. "I fail to see your meaning or your gift."

"Patience, lady. You will see it soon enough." He held out the branch to Titania.

"Fool! Do you think I should be so dimwitted as to accept a gift from you?"

"If you will not take my gift then I must force you to accept it," Tamlin said as he flung the branch at her feet. Then, quickly, more quickly than Titania thought possible, Tamlin became a hawk again.

As she watched him soar toward the horizon, she detected a change in the atmosphere. Something was happening. The sky became dark and ominous, clouds roiling overhead.

He thinks this will impress me?

"Tamlin," she called, taunting him. "You woke me up for this? A storm? If you only knew how dull these sullen little dramas make you. How predictable you've become. You think—"

This is no storm, she realized with growing

horror. As she gazed out over her kingdom, the very lands themselves shriveled, writhed, and died. Her beautiful green grass faded into a dry, dusty brown. The trees in the orchards, their limbs laden with glorious bounty, were suddenly bare, the fruit rotten and petrifying on the patchy ground.

Realizing that the "truth" he brought her was represented by the stick, she kicked the twig violently.

"Is this your gift to me, my love?" she shrieked to the darkening skies. "Is this your truth? This devastation?"

She sank, weeping, to her knees. She clutched the marble railing, leaning her head against it for support. "How could you do this?" she moaned. "*I* may have brought you sorrow, but the *land* brought you only peace. I cannot understand you, Tamlin."

She threw back her head defiantly. "But know this," she declared to the air. "Faerie's reach is long. You'll find no haven. You will tell us why you have murdered Faerie . . . before you die."

The Queen's voice faded as Tamlin made the arduous journey across worlds. His thoughts were full of Timothy Hunter as he soared above the gray London skyline.

If you had a child of heart and spirit, with the

potential for power, Tamlin thought, *and you wished to confine him to a prison where his heart's fire would be trapped and his spirit's wings would shrivel, and you sought to ensure that his potential would remain potential only, you could do no better than to leave him in this city.*

Tamlin was not one for cement, high-rises, and caverns created by steel towers. The noxious fumes spewing from the urban setting made his wings feel heavy with soot and grime.

Tamlin alighted on a tree outside Timothy Hunter's window, his talons clinging to a snowy branch. His sharp movements sent shivers of snow to the ground. *But be it in heaven or hell or any of the thousand realms between, no prison can truly cage a child of earth if the spirit of the child lives,* Tamlin thought. He remained perched in his spot, observing Timothy Hunter.

You've known deprivation, child, Tamlin reflected, *but have you ever suffered true hunger, endured real thirst? Sheltered as you are, what have you ever had to fear? What have you ever loved and fought for, won or lost? What can you know of courage?*

What are you, Timothy Hunter, and what must I do to wake you?

Chapter Five

TIM MADE IT BACK ALIVE from the strange
desert, and no one had even noticed that he had
been gone. School was school, Dad was Dad.
Coach Michelson was the tiniest bit nicer to him.
That was the only thing that had changed. Molly
was absent the day he returned, and although he
didn't have to face her after his ridiculous display
on the field, he missed having her to talk to.

   After school, Tim sat up in his room, writing
in his journal.

Today at school old Henderson said that
no one really knows what holds the world
together. And nobody knows why every-
thing doesn't just fall apart. And the
weird bit is that the stuff that DOES fall
apart, falls apart because it's not moving.

As long as those molecules and atoms keep zipping around, everything's dandy. But stop and—kapowie. It's all over.

Old Henderson calls that entropy.

Maybe that's what's wrong with Dad. He stopped moving when Mom died. So now he's falling apart. Because of entropy.

I think it really comes down to love and fear. Only nobody talks about love and fear in science. Love could be the stuff that keeps things moving so they stay together. Fear is the stuff that makes things hold so still they fall apart. And sometimes you can have both of them inside you, pushing and pulling you around and that's when you cry or laugh. Dad cries and laughs when he's watching telly. That's what the telly is about, mostly. Somebody trying to make you cry or laugh.

Tim read over his entry. *Well, that sounds stupid,* he thought. Gripping his pencil, he added, *I don't know what holds the bloody world together. Unless it's magic.*

He put down his journal. He needed to move; he was too restless to stay cooped up inside.

"I'm going out for a bit," he called to his dad as he headed for the front door.

"Don't stay out too late," his father replied, never taking his eyes from the television. Dad was obviously back to his same old self.

The door banged shut behind him. Timothy wandered through a snowy London. The weather had turned brisk and chill—a far cry from that desert wasteland he'd been taken to.

What was that all about? Tim wondered. *How did I manage to get home?* He fingered the amulet he had in his pocket—the stone that Tamlin had given him. *What did that bloke mean, that I was somehow the key to healing Faerie? How could that be possible?*

If I can magic myself home, why can't I magic Yo-yo back to me? Clearly there are volumes I don't know about magic.

Tim came across a deep imprint in the snow. "Oh, poor angel," Tim said. "I don't suppose you'll be going anywhere with those wings. They're a bit too small for flying, don't you think?" He studied the stunted snow angel. "I don't know how anyone could have gone and left you like that. All mutated looking and all. But they did."

Tim considered lying down in the snow to

create a greater wingspan for the snow angel, then decided against it. He'd look a daft fool. Snow angels were for little kids.

He wandered further. He peered into the window of a pet store, looking at the woeful puppies, their big eyes begging to be claimed. "Sorry, little fellas," he said to the puppies. "Me and my dad can barely take care of ourselves. No sense in bringing a puppy into that environment."

He heard a loud clang behind him, and all the puppies started barking hysterically. Tim turned to see an enormous hawk perched on an iron fence nearby.

Tim backed up against the pet store window. The bird was huge and powerful, and it gazed at him unblinking. It sent shivers of recognition through Tim.

"You," Tim declared. "It *is* you, isn't it? Where are your knives and nets and creepo sidekicks? Are they out lurking in the snow somewhere?"

The bird stared, silent.

"What do you want with me this time?" Tim demanded. "Another test? Well, get lost. Leave me alone."

The bird lifted off and flew away.

Tim stared after the bird, surprised that it had listened to him. Then he regretted sending it away.

He dashed after the bird. "You could at least

have told me what you wanted," he called up to it.

He followed the hawk to a parklike square with benches and trees and bits of snow-covered lawn. The soaring bird circled, landed, then to Tim's amazement, transformed into a man.

A *naked* man!

Tamlin.

"It *is* you," Tim exclaimed. Then, blushing, he glanced around. "Err. Turning into birds is one thing. But you can't just walk around London naked. Even if it weren't freezing outside."

"That's why we're here. Come with me."

"You think you can find a wardrobe in the park?" Tim asked. Everything had once again turned seriously strange.

A few yards away a homeless man sat on a bench surrounded by shopping bags. The man wore a battered khaki jacket with lots of badges pinned to it. His nose was pierced, and his thick full beard was gray and white. He had a scarf wrapped around his bald head, and thick newspapers were tied around his feet instead of shoes. His arms were crossed over his chest, and he rubbed them to stay warm.

"Good morning, Kenny," Tamlin greeted the man. "Can you lend me something to wear?"

So this bird-man from Faerie knows a homeless bloke in London. Tim thought. *Why not?*

"Aww, no, no, my friend." Kenny's voice was rough and gravelly, as if he weren't used to speaking. "Where would I be now if I was lending things away all the time? It's all about business. You have been away so long you have forgotten. This world will suck the juice out of you if you lose sight of business."

"Then we will come to terms," Tamlin replied.

Kenny rummaged through one of his shopping bags and pulled out a pile of rumpled clothes. He held them out to Tamlin. "Don't put on those socks until I find you some shoes." Kenny went back to searching through his bags. "You're a boot man, aren't you?"

To Tim, the bags didn't look large enough to hold men's boots, but Kenny produced a pair. "Now let me tell you what I want," he told Tamlin as the hawk man pulled on the boots. "I have had enough of being snowed on today. I need a respite from this weather."

"Ask Tim," Tamlin said, lacing up his boots. "He's the magician."

"What?" Tim asked, surprised. "Are you suggesting I do something about the weather? Me?"

"You may know nothing, boy, but you're no less a magician for all that."

Tim's hackles rose. Did Tamlin say he was stupid? Sure, Tim himself had just been thinking how little he knew about magic, but it was one thing for Tim to think that about himself and quite another for Tamlin to say it!

"Magic is *in* you," Tamlin continued. "And magic responds to need. Not your need alone. Anyone's."

"Now you sound like some mad New Ager," Tim scoffed.

"And you sound angry," Tamlin countered. "Why? Because I said you know nothing? Be angry with me then, but look. Look at Kenny." Tamlin placed a hand on Tim's shoulder. Tim braced himself for more rough handling, but he felt only a strong guiding hand turning him to face the homeless man. "Kenny is old. You wouldn't believe me if I told you how old."

"I might," Tim muttered.

"He's mad as a March hare but he's a good man. And he's cold."

Tim looked at Kenny. Now that Tamlin had pointed it out, he saw that Kenny *was* old. And on top of that, his teeth were chattering, his skin was taking on a bluish hue, and his shoulders were hunched up around his ears. The chubby old guy had given Tamlin what he needed, and all he wished for was to be warm. Tim wanted to help him, but how?

Tim looked up at the sky. The snow was

falling even harder now. It was beautiful but chilling. *Strange how something so pretty could make someone so unhappy*, Tim thought. He could feel his hair getting damp, and his toes tingled as the snow seeped into his shoes. Kenny must be truly miserable with his newspaper-swaddled feet and thin jacket.

But what could *he* do about it? Changing the weather was an impossible request. Tim held out his arms. "Look at all this snow. I can't!"

Tamlin released Tim's shoulder and stepped back. "How would you know what you can or can't do without trying? When was the last time you attempted anything that could embarrass you?"

This took Tim aback. What was Tamlin talking about? Then he remembered—he'd run out of the football game because he had felt humiliated in front of Molly. He wouldn't even try for the ball for fear he'd make a fool of himself. A little while ago he had wanted to lie down in the snow and extend that snow angel's imprint, but wouldn't let himself because he didn't want to seem like a foolish kid. How many other things did he avoid doing just because he was afraid of making a mistake— or being laughed at?

How long had Tamlin been watching him?

There was a challenge in Tamlin, but it wasn't a cruel challenge. He wasn't taunting him.

Somehow Tim knew that even if he made a whopping mistake, he wouldn't be laughed at—he'd be encouraged to try again. Tim sensed that, in an oblique way, Tamlin was trying to help him take some kind of step forward.

"Okay!" Tim declared. He shut his eyes and held out his arms wide. *Go away snow*, he thought. Nothing. *Snow, begone!* The snow was still falling. For good measure, he added fancier words—this was magic, after all—*Snow goeth far from here. I banish thee, snow, to . . . to . . . to wherever it is that snow comes from*.

It was no use. The snow was still landing on his hair, his face. His shoulders slumped as he lowered his arms, defeated. He couldn't meet Tamlin's eyes, afraid he'd see disappointment there. "I—I did try," he said.

"Yes, you did," Tamlin said. "I could feel your effort." Tamlin's voice was gentle. Tim felt the man's hand on his back. "Now tell me this: If I told you I was thirsty, would you fetch me a river?"

Tim glanced up at Tamlin's face. "That's a stupid question. Of course not."

Tamlin smiled.

Tim smiled back as he understood what Tamlin was saying. "Ohhh," Tim said.

Tamlin nodded back. "There's no need to carry a river, is there? Not when a cup will do.

Now, try again. I'll help you."

Tim was eager to try again. He faced Kenny, uncertain of how to start.

"Lace crystals are falling everywhere," Tamlin said. "Feel them."

Tim concentrated, allowing himself to truly feel the snow as separate, delicate things instead of a massive clump of wet cold.

"They drift down, feathered wheels of ice," Tamlin crooned.

Nothing was happening. It was too hard. "They're everywhere," Tim protested. "How can I do anything about that?"

"Not everywhere," Tamlin corrected. "Between them there is space. Space curls between them, dances above and around and below them. Take that space. Feel it. Shape it."

Tim felt his hands rise unbidden, as if there were energy coursing through him, guiding them. He sensed the air between the ice crystals. He forced the space to open up, spreading the feathered wheels of frozen water apart. He never touched the flakes themselves with his mind; instead he worked on the space in between, just as Tamlin said.

He saw Kenny grin. "That is a fine boy you have there, Tamlin. Take care of him."

Tim's jaw dropped. Snow was still falling all

around, but none was falling on Kenny. It was as if Kenny moved in a protective bubble that the snow could not break through.

Excited, Tim turned to Tamlin. "Did you—"

"Did I help you?" Tamlin grinned. "No."

"I— It felt like—like tying a knot but not with my hands."

"You did well, Tim. Very well."

It felt great to hear this strong and self-contained man say that.

"What you've done, you've done with your own power," Tamlin assured him. "That binding was your work, not mine."

Tim could not contain the broad smile spreading across his face. Pride of accomplishment made his skin tingle with warmth despite the snow. *I did it*, he thought. *Incredible. I did it for real. I worked magic. I made something happen.*

"Tam," Kenny said. "If you want the accessories, you come get them." He held out a hat and a leather gauntlet. "It was some trouble finding the right things," he added, "but I would not want you to feel cheated."

Tim wondered what was going on. How could Kenny have known what Tamlin would need? Did he know that Tamlin was going to show up in London naked?

Tamlin looked down at the hat in Kenny's

outstretched hands but made no move to take it.
Tim stamped his feet to keep warm. *What's taking
so long?* It couldn't be because Tamlin didn't like
the hat Kenny had picked out for him. Tim didn't
imagine Tamlin was concerned about style.

"Don't you crook those eyebrows at me, old
bird," Kenny scolded. "This is just the hat for
you. Sure as oysters have pearls. So take it and
motivate yourself out of here. Fast, my friend.
Fast as you can."

"I'll take the hat and the gauntlet. That's all,"
Tamlin said. "Not the gun."

Gun? Tim's head whipped around. Tamlin was
placing the hat on his head while Kenny slipped
something into one of the many shopping bags
that surrounded him. Why would Kenny have
offered Tamlin a gun?

"Wh-what's going on?" Tim asked.

Tamlin strode toward him, slung an arm over
Tim's shoulder, and started him walking. "It's
time for us to go."

Tim craned his neck, trying to look back at
Kenny. "You didn't even tell him good-bye."

"Tim. Come. Now."

Uh-oh. The Trenchcoat Brigade had sometimes spoken to him in that same brusque
manner. It usually meant someone was about to
try to kill him.

Tamlin picked up speed, and Tim wondered if they were being followed—and if Tamlin had a destination in mind.

Before Tim took another step, he wanted answers. He dug in his heels and skidded to a stop. "Just a minute," he said. "You still haven't told me why you came back here. I want to know. What do you want with me?"

Tamlin stopped walking, turned, and faced Tim. His expression was serious, but he said nothing.

"The first time I met you, you kidnapped me and threatened me," Tim continued. "You dumped me in some weird desert and flew off. And now you turn up and you—"

"Tim—" Tamlin cut him off. "Listen to me. It's dangerous to stay in one place too long. I haven't the time to explain myself fully to you here and now. I can only tell you I have come to seek your help."

"My help?" Tim could not imagine what this powerful, intense man could need from him. "Why?"

"Because Faerie is dying."

Tim remembered that Tamlin had said this to him before. When the man had kidnapped him and dragged him off to the desert he had told Tim that the land was dying. *But how can an entire world die*? Faerie was so beautiful, so full of life. *Though if that desert really was Faerie it certainly looked like it was in bad shape*, Tim thought.

But even if that were true . . . "How can I help? I'm just a kid."

"You are much more than that, child, and I believe you know that," Tamlin said. He sighed. "For you to truly understand you need to know everything."

Finally, Tim thought. *Now we're getting somewhere.*

"Once my world and yours were one. The lives of the Fair Folk and the lives of mortals intertwined and were interdependent. But there was a severing of those ties. A walling off. Because of that, Faerie withers."

Suddenly, a tiny winged creature appeared and fluttered between Tim and Tamlin. "You are the master of understatement, Tamlin," the creature said. "The place looks very much like hell."

Tim took several startled steps backward. The creature was the size of the pretty little flitlings he had seen in Faerie at the Queen's court. But this creature wasn't pretty. He looked wild—with ragged auburn hair, pointed ears, and long sharp fingers. His wings were translucent, like a dragonfly's, and his eyes were angular and shifty. He wore a colorful loincloth and had a muscular body, though he was no bigger than

Tamlin's hand.

"Amadan," Tamlin said.

"In the flesh." He gave a bow and grinned up at Tim. Tim smiled back. Okay, Amadan was kind of cute. The creature darted over to Tim and hovered at eye level.

"I am a Fool," Amadan said, "a court jester. And when the occasion warrants, a messenger. Anything to make milady smile, eh, Tamlin?"

Amadan landed on Tim's shoulder, and balanced himself by tugging on Tim's ear.

"Hey!" Tim protested.

Amadan ignored Tim and settled himself inside the neck of Tim's jacket. The creature's sharp toes tickled.

"Alas, our most gracious Queen is difficult to amuse at present," Amadan said. Tim could feel the creature's breath on his neck. It was surprisingly cold. "I would not say she pines for you, Tamlin, but it does seem certain she'd take pleasure in your company."

"Tim," Tamlin ordered sternly. "Don't move. Hold very still."

Tim gulped. Tamlin's worry scared him. He could now feel little Amadan gripping his throat with his talons. Did the flitling realize its own strength?

Tamlin held up his hand in a placating gesture.

"Amadan, there is no need for you to—"

"You're interrupting me," Amadan snapped. "Grave discourtesy to a messenger. At the risk of discomfiting you I must insist, Tamlin, that you come with me to Faerie."

Now Tim felt Amadan's fingers lengthen and grow into razor-sharp claws. For one so tiny, Amadan's grip was powerful. He was beginning to crush Tim's Adam's apple, as he scraped the skin on Tim's neck.

"Stop," Tim choked out.

"So, Tamlin, you will accompany me to Faerie. You'll swear by oak and ash and thorn to attend milady's pleasure there."

"He's hurting me," Tim whispered. It was all the sound he could muster. The pressure on his throat was intense.

"If you don't," Amadan hissed, "I'll do something memorable and picturesque to the boy."

Out of the corner of his eye Tim was horrified to see Amadan transform from an impish elf to a nasty-looking creature with a skull-like face and rows of sharp teeth.

"Make him stop, please," Tim begged hoarsely.

Amadan yanked back Tim's head as if he were going to gnaw his way through Tim's neck with those gnashing fangs. "Well?"

"I swear," Tamlin agreed. "Release the boy

unhurt and let him go free. And by oak and thorn and ash I will return with you to Faerie. I will surrender to your mistress."

Amadan gave a little laugh. "I thought you would." He flew out of Tim's jacket and hung in the air above Tim's head.

Tim rubbed his neck and swallowed a few times, trying to get his throat back in working order.

"Tim, make the most of your time in this world," Tamlin said sadly. "Always remember, in life as in magic, power resides in little things. And in truth."

Tim stared at the man. These sounded like parting words of advice—the kind grown-ups gave if they thought they weren't going to see you again.

"How very touching," Amadan sneered. "Come, Falconer. We've kept milady waiting long enough."

"Farewell," Tamlin said, placing a hand on Tim's shoulder.

"Wait." Tim gripped Tamlin's arm. "What you said. You can't have meant it." Tim swallowed. It hurt to speak. "You aren't going to get drawn and quartered or something just because—just because . . ."

Tamlin said nothing. He simply vanished. Right out of Tim's grasp. He was there one minute, and then he seemed to dissolve into a wisp and was gone. So was Amadan.

Tim dropped to his knees in the snow. "You were afraid he'd hurt me," Tim murmured. "And I whimpered and begged." Shame colored Tim's pale cheeks red and choked him worse than Amadan's claws. "And now you're in trouble. You said you came here for my help. Instead I've gone and gotten you in deep."

"Do not worry too much about your father."

Tim looked up to see Kenny the homeless man standing over him. "What?"

"Are you deaf, lad? I said, don't worry about your father. He's always been in trouble, and he always will be. It's in the blood. But then I expect you know that by now."

Tim looked puzzled. "What's Dad got to do with this? He wouldn't know danger from . . ." Then Tim paused. He realized Kenny was staring at him, smiling.

"Wait a minute—you're not talking about Dad at all. . . . Are you saying—are you trying to say Tamlin's—?"

Kenny trudged away, still in the snow-free zone Tim had created.

Tim sat there in the snow, stunned.

"My father?"

Chapter Six

Tɪᴍ ᴡᴀɴᴅᴇʀᴇᴅ ᴛʜᴇ sᴛʀᴇᴇᴛs hunched up against the cold. He didn't know where he was walking or where he was going, only that he needed to keep moving. His mind was racing at top speed.

If your dad wasn't really your dad, you'd have figured it out yourself, Tim told himself. *By the time you were six or seven, if you weren't totally clueless, you would have known. Just known!*

Tim's feet stamped hard, leaving squashed footsteps behind. The snow had stopped falling and the wind had picked up, making it bitterly cold. Tim felt nothing.

If you've never doubted that your father was your father—not even once in your life—that has to mean something, doesn't it?

No one looks exactly like his parents. Tim thought about the boys at school. *Bobby Saunders doesn't look a thing like his dad. And Brian Hyde and his dad don't look much alike, until you start to notice little things.*

Little things. Wasn't that what Tamlin had just told him to look for?

Maybe it's not the color of your hair that you get from your father. Maybe it's the shape of your nose, your walk, or your general attitude. Or it could be your body type. Whether you're a mesomorph or an endomorph, or whatever the other morph is.

He had arrived at a door. Molly's door. This was where his feet had brought him, as his brain spun around and around in a dizzying fashion. Tim's hand reached out without instruction and he rang the bell.

He could hear loud shouts and a baby crying behind the door, then footsteps. He looked up so that he could be viewed through the little peephole in the door, and he heard the locks being undone. The door swung open.

"Hey, Tim," Molly greeted. She wore blue sweatpants and a baggy sweatshirt, and her feet were bare. He noticed each of her toenails was painted a different color, as if she wanted to make a rainbow of her feet. "What are you doing here?"

"What's the other morph, Molly?" Tim asked.

She cocked her head to one side, her dark hair falling across her shoulder. Without missing a beat, she asked, "Do you mean like in the sci-fi pictures, when the bad guy morphs into another creature?"

"No, like we learned at school. Endomorph, mesomorph, and . . . and I can't think of the other one."

Molly laughed and placed her hands on her hips. "Timothy Hunter. You came here at dinner-time in the snow to ask me a biology question? Are you mad?"

Tim ducked his chin and stared down at his trainers. He knew he sounded stupid—daft even. He started to turn to leave.

He felt Molly's hand on his shoulder. "No, you're not mad, but you're not all right either. I can see." She jerked her head toward the living room. "Come on, then. In with you. Can't have you moping around worrying about ectomorphs in that cold."

She stepped aside so he could enter. "And it is ectomorphs." She brushed some snowflakes from the shoulder of his jacket. "I'm surprised you didn't remember that one, Tim. It's what you are. Naturally thin."

She led him through the living room into the kitchen. Molly had a big family. Tim wasn't exactly sure how many of them there were, since there were often relatives with their own children staying, and sometimes Molly's parents were gone for stretches at a time. There was a baby in a highchair—he recognized her as Molly's little sister Krista. There were three dirty boys ranging in age from two through about seven, a fat man in an undershirt eating a bowl of spaghetti, and a skinny lady at the stove. The skinny, sad-looking lady was Molly's mum, but the fat man was a stranger to Tim.

"Mum, Tim's here. Can we eat up in my room?" Molly asked.

"Suit yourself," Molly's mother replied. She dished out a bowl for Molly and one for Tim. "Remember to bring the plates back downstairs." She handed the bowl to Tim. "Nice to see you, Timothy." She nodded toward the fat man. "This here is my brother Patrick, Molly's uncle."

The man nodded a greeting at Tim but didn't raise his eyes from the newspaper he was reading.

"Hello," Tim said.

"Come on," Molly urged. She bounded up the stairs and into her room. Tim followed her inside and shut the door.

Molly shuddered. "Families," she said. "Can't live with 'em, can't come into the world without 'em."

"Yeah . . ." Tim stared down at his bowl of pasta and sauce. "Yeah." Although he felt all empty inside, he knew it wasn't from hunger. He placed the bowl on Molly's messy desk, then sat on the floor, his back against her unmade bed.

"Tim?" Molly sat on the floor beside him. "What's wrong? Is it about what happened at school the other day?"

Tim peered at her. "At school?"

"You know. You raced off the field like that, Coach Michelson calling after you. Did you get into trouble?"

Tim rubbed his face. The football scrimmage seemed so remote, so unimportant now. "I guess I got into trouble. Coach Michelson called my dad. I mean . . ."

"Timothy Hunter. You tell me what is going on with you right now," Molly demanded. "You came here for a reason, and I don't think it was for pasta from a tin."

Tim brought his knees up and lay his arms across them. How could he start? How could he even say the words? He could feel Molly waiting. He badly needed to work this out, but it was so huge. Huger even than the whole magic thing. It was too scary to contemplate alone. He needed her, but to get her to help him he would have to produce words, and that seemed incredibly hard to do. Impossible, really.

He shut his eyes. Maybe if he pretended he

was just talking to himself it would be easier. Sometimes it was as comfortable as talking to himself when he was with Molly. She reflected him, like a mirror, but with an opinion and point of view of her own. *Try*, he told himself. *Like Tamlin said, don't stop yourself for fear of being embarrassed*. He was afraid his voice would crack, that he might cry or shout. He was afraid of being a fool, but he had to be willing to risk humiliation to be able to do great things.

Not that this was any great thing. But it was a great *big* thing.

"Tim." Molly's voice was gentle but insistent. "You'll feel better. You know you will."

"I—I found out today . . ." Tim cleared his throat and started again. "I have reason to believe that my father is not actually my father," he blurted.

He couldn't look at her. He heard her take in a surprised breath, then felt her hand on his ankle. "No wonder you're wrecked. That's major."

Tim looked at her. "Am I that stupid? How could I not have known?"

"We believe what our parents tell us," Molly said. "It's what kids do. That's why it's so easy for grown-ups to lie to us."

Tim thought she sounded sad, as if there were times she had believed her parents when she shouldn't have.

"Besides, what kind of clues would there have been?" Molly offered. "What could have told you any different? Hey, it's only lately that you even figured out the, you know, facts of life. And until you knew the biology of it, why would you question it?" Molly laughed. "So this was a biology question, after all."

Tim shook his head but grinned. "I suppose I should have studied more then."

"So what does your dad say about all this?" Molly asked.

Tim gave her a sideways look. "Which one?"

Molly shoved his knees a little. "You know. The one who bugs you about your homework every night. The one you complain about incessantly. That dad."

"Oh, him." Tim lay his head on his knees. He shut his eyes. He didn't know whether he should be angry at his dad or feel sorry for him. Did his father even know that he wasn't—well, his father? Was this some sort of huge secret Tim was now burdened with? He turned his head and squinted at Molly. "I don't know."

"He wasn't the one who told you?" Now Molly's dark eyes were wide with surprise. "Then how —"

Tim raised a hand to interrupt her. "Long story. Don't ask."

"How do you know it's true?" Molly asked.

Tim lifted his head and stared straight ahead. Molly had a point. She usually did. Wasn't a person supposed to get—what was the term they used in the action pictures—corroborating evidence? After all, who had hit him with this news flash? Kenny the homeless stranger. Not exactly a reliable source.

But Tim knew he was so rattled because he *sensed* this to be the truth. He had felt something like kinship, some unnameable connection, with Tamlin. A kinship that might be explained if they were actually kin.

"Talk to your dad," Molly urged. "Don't just take someone else's word for it. It's better to have things out in the open. Things fester in the dark. You'll feel better if you know all you can know."

Tim nodded. He knew she was right. He slowly unfolded himself from the floor and kicked out the kinks in his legs. He had walked a lot in the cold, and his body felt like he'd been run over by a train in the Underground. All his muscles hurt.

He gave Molly a sad grin. "Can't you ask him about it for me?"

"Sorry. This is one you've got to do on your own."

"I was afraid of that."

"It might be all right," Molly said.

"How could it possibly be all right?" Tim asked.

"I used to always imagine my parents weren't my real parents," Molly said, flopping down on her bed. She lay on her back with her arms behind her head. She gazed up at the ceiling, a dreamy expression on her face. "I'd be the daughter of a pirate and an explorer."

Tim sat on the edge of the bed. "Who was who?"

"They alternated. Sometimes my dad was the pirate, sometimes my mum. But they were always so much more exciting than my real parents. Nicer, too," she added softly.

Tim's brow crinkled. Tamlin was certainly a more exciting figure than his beer-swigging, telly-watching dad. He wasn't particularly nicer, though. Tim wasn't really sure what Tamlin was. The bloke was occasionally a bird, after all. *I mean, what does* that *tell you?*

Molly rolled over onto her side and propped herself up on her elbow. "You know, ultimately it doesn't matter, does it?"

Startled, Tim asked, "What do you mean?"

"Well, at the end of the day, you're still you, aren't you? No matter who your father is."

Tim shook his head but didn't reply. She

didn't seem to understand that this was precisely the point: If he could figure out who his father really was, that would give Tim clues about his own identity. Wouldn't it?

"Maybe bringing this secret to light will wake your dad up." Molly sat back up. "You know, change things between you."

"That's sort of what I'm afraid of," Tim said. "It could change everything. Molly, what if he doesn't know?" The thought of this made his heart hurt for his dad.

Molly gripped his hands. "Truth is always best. Remember that."

"I'll try." Tim paused a moment. "Are you sure you can't—"

Molly got off the bed and shoved Tim toward the door. "Go," she ordered. "And ring me the minute you're done talking."

Tim left the house, depositing his bowl of uneaten spaghetti on the kitchen drainboard on the way out. It was bitter cold outside now, and depending upon the state his father—Mr. Hunter—was in, he might catch it for being late and not phoning.

Maybe it was all a stupid prank, Tim thought as he jogged home. How could it be true? How could Tamlin be his father, anyway? *I mean, how would that have been possible?*

Tim charged into the house, scooting past his dad and the telly. He dashed up to his dad's bedroom and rummaged through the dresser drawers. He needed proof, evidence, something to tell him for dead certain who he was—where he had come from.

"Tim, what are you doing in that mess?" Mr. Hunter demanded from the doorway. Tim hadn't even heard him come upstairs.

"Looking," Tim said, rifling through some school papers and certificates.

"Looking for what, I'd like to know."

What am *I looking for?* Tim sank back onto his heels. He'd been looking for verification—but had no idea what form that would take. One possibility occurred to him. "Pictures of you. When you were my age." Maybe then he'd find a resemblance. It would be easier to see, if Tim could compare himself with his father before his dad had gone all soft and sad.

His father stepped into the room. "Well, I don't have any, and if I did, they wouldn't be in there, so just— Put that down," he suddenly ordered.

Tim looked down at the paper in his hands. It seemed to have upset his dad. It must be important. "What?" he asked. "It's just your marriage certificate. Yours and Mum's."

Tim peered closer at it. *Why would my finding*

this bother Dad so much? Then he noticed something that didn't make sense. "This says you got married in January." Tim turned to look at his dad. "But my birthday is in June."

"Yes," his father said carefully. "Quite so."

Tim stood up. "I did better in math than I did in biology. I can do the sums here. Mum was already pregnant with me when you got married." Tim felt a rushing sensation as all the blood hurried up to his head. His ears pounded, and he thought he could hear the sea. He turned and darted out of the room.

"Tim, don't go!" his father cried behind him. "It's not what you think! I loved your mother. I *wanted* to marry her. She was—"

Tim heard his father's voice break. It shocked him into freezing halfway down the stairs. He turned around and stared at his father. "Go on," Tim said, his voice low. "She was what?"

"She was wonderful. Too good for this world, I used to think." Mr. Hunter hung his head. "Too good for me, anyway." He looked up at Tim again, nervously fiddling with the keys in his trouser pocket. He gave a sad smile. "Her getting pregnant. That was a bit of luck, the way I saw it. I'm not sure your mother would have married me if she didn't think she had to."

Does he know? Tim searched his father's face

for an answer and didn't find it. _Does he know that I am not his child? Did my mother lead him to believe I was their child together so he would marry her?_

"I don't look like you," Tim said finally, not meeting his father's pained eyes. "Did you ever notice that?"

The distance between them—Tim halfway down the stairs and his father standing in the hall—was filled with such a fragile silence, the wrong answer could make it shatter.

"Yes," Mr. Hunter whispered. "It never mattered though." His voice got stronger. "It never mattered to me—ever."

Tim took that in; it was a relief in one way. His father hadn't been betrayed; his father had accepted things as they were. And yet . . .

Tim thought his head would explode. There were only more questions. Questions upon questions. He raced up the stairs, past his father, and slammed into his room.

Tim paced the tiny space. _When your father isn't really your father, and you don't catch on until you're thirteen, well, then, you're a bloody idiot, aren't you?_ Tim's hands balled into fists. He smacked them into his thighs. _What do I really know now? All I know is that the father I grew up with isn't my father at all._

He stopped in the center of the room and

rubbed his face, as if it would help him think. He felt determination rise up through the bewilderment. *So it's time to discover who my real father is. What kind of person would have done that? Knock up my mum and walk out of her life. And mine.*

Tim collapsed into his desk chair. His hands reached for the objects that lay strewn across his desk—a key, some coins, an amulet.

Tim picked up the key and turned it over and over in his hand. It had been given to him by Titania, Queen of Faerie, but it had almost cost him his freedom. When Titania suddenly tossed the key to him, Tim, forgetting the dangers of accepting a gift from one of the Fair Folk, had caught it. He had been excited when it turned out to be a key that opened doors to other worlds. He was less than thrilled when he was informed that, according to Faerie rules, catching it meant he would be required to stay there as the Queen's page. However, when Tim offered Titania his Mundane Egg in exchange—a gift of equal or greater value—the key became rightfully his, with no strings attached.

He shoved the key into his pocket. Then he picked up the amulet.

Maybe my father didn't walk *away. Maybe he* flew.

Tim held out the amulet Tamlin had given

him, staring at it hard. He recalled Tamlin's words. "Need, you said," he addressed the Opening Stone. "Magic answers need. All right. I need to know. I need to know now!"

Chapter Seven

QUEEN TITANIA WANDERED the grounds of
her castle. She felt weary, weighed down by grief.
The hem of her long lavender velvet dress trailed
through dead branches and leaves, but she ignored
it. What did it matter? What could matter now?

Tamlin had forced her to face the truth:
Faerie was dying. She had been shocked awake as
if he had tossed bracing cold water into her face.
How she wished he had not; she preferred the
cloaking glamours that kept her surrounded in
beauty.

But truth had arrived with a vengeance.
There was no avoiding the crumbled stones that
once were a splendid stairway, the tumbled tree,
or the withered vines. Try as she might, Titania
could not lift the pall over the lands, nor return
the sky's color from a murky, muddy gray to its
former clear and brilliant blue.

Titania stopped by the vine-covered wall that circled her estate. Where once there had been pink and scarlet roses, there were now brown and black twisted shapes unrecognizable as flowers, as if the life force had been choked from them. She reached out to stroke the decaying petals, but as gentle as her light touch was, it was too much for the petrified husks; they disintegrated into dust.

"Oh, my Faerie," she moaned. "You were the heart of me. If tears could restore you, then tears you would have—oceans of them."

She touched the vines again. "But tears will do nothing." She felt the prick of the thorns on her fingertips and gazed down at the droplets of blood as they appeared. "It may be *blood* that must be shed for you. For us."

She began her slow walk again. Anger began to cut through her sadness. *If it is blood you need, then blood it is*, she thought. *Blood of your murderer—blood of the man who was once my lover.*

Titania stopped walking. She could feel a presence forming behind her. It was time to have this out.

"Milady," Amadan said. "We two fools attend your pleasure."

Titania turned around to face them. The untrustworthy Fool and the man who had been her downfall. Tamlin.

"I thank you, my Amadan, for fulfilling my request with such speed," she said. "But do not speak to me of pleasure. Not here, not now." She addressed Tamlin. "You see your handiwork, Falconer?" Titania gestured at the barren trees, the dried and parched riverbed.

"I see it."

"And the sight gives you satisfaction?"

"I've been satisfied once or twice in my life," Tamlin answered evenly. It irked Titania to see him so calm. She wasn't rousing a reaction in him.

Tamlin sighed. "But that was long ago. This place was a paradise then, and you were—"

"I am what I have always been," Titania snapped. "But you . . ." She crossed her arms over her chest, her jeweled cuffs jangling as she brought them together. "Look at this creature, Amadan," she said disdainfully. "He was not always thus, but see him now. Don't let him fool you. He is not a man who takes pleasure in wearing a hawk's wings. He's a hawk who finds it useful to pretend he's a man. What do you say to that, my lord raptor?"

There. That should get a rise out of him. Her pain made her desperate to hurt him. Why was it not working?

"I say that you mask your thoughts with your words," Tamlin replied, "just as you concealed the truth of this garden with spells of glamour."

Titania's eyes flashed fury at this, but she was pleased to see the glint of anger in Tamlin's brown eyes. He took a step closer to her.

"Why don't you pick a peach from that beautiful tree, my lady?" He pointed to one of the few trees in the orchard that had not yet been overtaken by the blight. From Tamlin's tone, Titania knew that the tree's bounty was just illusion. "Take a big bite," he sneered.

Having broken through his implacability, his stone mask, Titania knew they would now speak to each other honestly. She wanted no witnesses for that. "Amadan, leave us."

The flitling hovered a moment, his eyes narrowed. Titania could see he resented being dismissed. *He really is becoming far too arrogant for safety*, Titania observed. She had leaned on him too long, too frequently, and too indiscriminately, particularly since she and Tamlin had grown so far apart. "Go," she said to Amadan.

He bowed in midair. "Yes, milady. What pleases milady, pleases me."

She fought the urge to swat Amadan for his insincerity. Did he think she did not see through him? But that problem would have to wait; she had other matters to deal with.

She watched Amadan fly away. She kept her

back to Tamlin; she didn't want him to see her vulnerability, and she didn't trust herself to be able to mask it. "Why, Tamlin?" she asked a little more piteously than she meant to. "Why have you made this gentle place a hell?" She tried to keep the desperate sadness from her voice but did not succeed.

"Lady, I did not create this desolation."

She whirled around. "I do not believe you."

"The realm has been withering for centuries," Tamlin shouted at her, suddenly furious. "You haven't seen it until now because you've chosen not to. All I did was open your eyes."

He gripped her upper arms. She was frightened to see the passion and pain in his face. She was shocked by the realization that he was as devastated by this as she was.

"Sarisen, a city I loved, is now a husk that desert winds howl through," he told her, his voice shaking. "Red sand has choked the life from the bejeweled caverns of Ulven."

Titania squirmed in his grip. She hated this directness, had lived her life avoiding it. Tamlin held her tightly and did not let go. "Riverbeds have gone dry, choking the fish so that they suffocate in agony. The bones of the hobble children bleach in the glare of the sun."

"Enough!" she cried out, tears streaming down her face. "What would you have me do?"

"Not do, lady. Undo." He released her, and she stumbled backward a few steps. She rubbed her arms where his hands had clasped her. Once he had done so only in love; now his aggressive touch was an accusation. An invasion.

"Tear down the walls you've raised," he said. His voice was pleading. "Open your twilight land fully to the world again. More than these tiny gaps that allow a few to slip in and out. Let it be now as it was in the beginning, when Faerie touched the Earthlands with her mystery, and in return they gave her life."

She stared at him. How did he know what she had done so long ago? Worse, he had no idea that what he was asking her to do was impossible. "You're mad."

"Am I? More than the land has changed since the Fair Folk withdrew from the world of mortal kind. You've changed—all of you. You've lost something. Lost it to fear."

She could not meet his eyes. She knew he was right, but she didn't know how to fix it. He mistook her silence for disagreement.

"When was the last time you laughed because you felt it, milady?" he demanded. "You speak constantly of pleasure, but when did you last know joy?"

She could take no more. She had to confess.

"Tamlin, stop. These things you say may well be true." She wrapped her arms around herself as if she were afraid she might shatter. She yearned for the comfort and safety she had once felt in Tamlin's strong embrace, but she knew that the time was long past.

"But I have already undone the bindings I wrought so long ago," she told him. "I learned recently that the woman, that Earth woman who held you in thrall, had died. When I finally saw Faerie in this state, I tried to reopen the portals, no longer fearing that I would lose you to her. It changed nothing."

He shook his head incredulously. "It was *jealousy* that made you do such a thing? Create the bindings between our world and theirs? Risk the life of all Faerie?"

"That doesn't matter now." She did not want him to dwell on that past. She needed him to understand her fear, the present crisis.

"Hear me," she said, taking a step toward him. "I told you—I undid what I had done. Do you understand? I told you that it changed nothing! I discovered other bindings. Choking our world tightly."

She gazed down at her feet and shook her head, answering his unasked question. "I do not know whose they are. But they are strong. Very strong. I cannot heal the breach I made between man's world and ours. Someone will not let me."

Now she searched his face, waiting for his response. He had to help her—help them all—help restore Faerie. But would he? Could he?

Tamlin nodded as if he were thinking it all through. "Then we need to find a different hope," he said finally.

Chapter Eight

TIM LOOKED AROUND HIM. "I—I—did it," he stammered. "But what exactly did I do?"

He stared down at the amulet he still clutched in his hands. *Did I do this magic, or did the stone do it?* Tim wondered. No matter. He was . . . somewhere. But where?

He was someplace totally new. "Nothing recognizable here," he murmured. This wasn't the beautiful countryside he remembered from his first trip to Faerie. It wasn't the desolate desert where Tamlin, his maybe father, had brought him. This was someplace . . . twisted. He could feel it. It even smelled wrong—sort of like the garbage when he and his dad forgot to take it out for a few days.

Tim shoved the stone back into his pocket, then gazed around. He was standing in a broken-down courtyard of a mansion that had seen better days. A brick wall surrounded the grounds, making it impossible for Tim to see what lay beyond it. As his eyes traveled up the wall he noticed the sky was a bruised purple. *Is it going to storm*, Tim wondered, *or does it always look like that here?*

Tim took a step and heard a crunching sound. Glancing down, he discovered he was standing on a pile of skeletons. He lifted his foot and carefully placed it a few inches over, in the nearest clear space, then gingerly brought his other foot beside it.

Tim fought back a shudder. Skulls with their gaping eye sockets stared back at him, and the entire courtyard was littered with rib cages, leg bones, and skeletons of creatures Tim didn't recognize.

"Great," he muttered, "I've landed in bone city."

Looking down at the little pile beside him, Tim was horrified to see that the bones were covered with teeth marks. These creatures didn't just die here—they were someone—or some*thing*'s meal.

I don't think this is where I want to be, Tim decided. He scanned the wall. *That doesn't seem too tough. Shouldn't be any harder than scaling the walls at the car park.* But back home in London the wall around the car park was designed to keep him out. Tim had a sinking feeling that here the wall was intended to keep him in.

Tim picked his way over to the wall, trying to avoid crunching any more of the scattered bones, but they were hard to avoid. He cringed every time he heard another crack.

He reached as high as he could up the wall and shoved his fingers in between the crumbling bricks. With a grunt, he pulled himself up. Feeling along the wall, he found a handhold, then bent his leg until his foot found a toehold. By straightening his leg and pulling hard with his arms, he lifted himself another foot up the wall.

That's it, he told himself. *Piece o' cake.*

He repeated the process: handhold, foothold, grunt, up. Sometimes his progress was mere inches. Sometimes he covered more ground. Each time, he scraped his knuckles, his knees, his face.

Sweat poured down his back. *I've got to be near the top by now,* he thought. Tim squinted up. He blinked several times, certain his eyes must be playing tricks on him.

How is that possible? The top of the wall seemed as far away now as it had been when he had started.

It didn't seem to be much of a wall from the ground, he thought, gritting his teeth and reaching again. *Only fifteen or twenty feet high. With lots of cracks and little ledge things to hang on to.*

He let out a groan. His shoulders burned from the effort, and his arms felt wobbly as his muscles grew exhausted.

It looked like an easy climb. Just one problem. You can't ever get to the top.

"Harum." Tim heard someone clear his throat below him. "I venture to suggest that you are unacquainted with Zeno's paradox, or you'd be exerting yourself to better purpose."

Tim craned his neck to glance down. A man in a velvet overcoat, a ruffled shirt, and breeches looked up at him. His greasy red hair fell limply from his receding forehead to his high stiff collar. From his spot halfway up the wall, Tim couldn't quite make out the man's face, but he could tell that there was something strange about it.

"Come down, my boy. And we will begin your education with this morsel of classical thought."

The man's voice was high-pitched, as if he were whining or his nose were too small. He also carried a riding crop, but he wasn't dressed for riding.

Seriously weird, Tim surmised.

"I think . . . I think I'd rather not," Tim replied. He faced the bricks and went back to trying to make it to the top of the wall.

The man below him cleared his throat again. "Harrum. Then we will begin your studies now. The paradox, as it is traditionally presented, involves the swift-footed Achilles and a tortoise. However, we can as easily illustrate Zeno's point with a boy and a wall. Are you listening, child?"

Suddenly, the man was above him, standing on top of the wall. Tim was so startled he nearly lost his grip. *How did he do that?*

The man knelt down, balancing himself with his riding crop. "Our boy climbs halfway up the wall. Eager to reach freedom, he continues to climb, and he covers half the remaining distance. And then half of that. But still some distance remains between the boy and his goal. So the boy climbs on and on, although his arms are tiring."

The man seemed to be in no hurry to get to the end of his story. Tim's fingers clung desperately to the rough bricks. *Why doesn't this creep hurry up and finish his stupid lecture? Or maybe,* Tim suspected, *he's taking so long in the hope that I'll lose my hold and drop back down.*

"The boy looks up," the man continued in his annoying, whiny voice, "and being quite a clever lad, he finally realizes that each time he covers only half the distance. Half, and then half of that, and then half of that. He is always halfway to freedom. Achilles never overtakes the tortoise.

The boy can never scale the wall. I'm afraid you're about to fall, child," the man said, suddenly leaning forward. "Perhaps you ought to take my hand."

"You wish!" Tim exclaimed. Recoiling from the man's outstretched palm, Tim lost his grip and tumbled to the ground. To his astonishment, the man was there to greet him.

Tim scrambled back up to his feet—he didn't want this jerk to see that he was rattled. Brushing off his jeans, he tried to regain his composure. "I know some of the rules, you know," Tim informed the creep. "I'm not about to take any favors from you. Or gifts. Or anything."

There, Tim thought, setting his jaw, *that should put the bloke in his place. Let him know what's what. I mean, he's not dealing with any ordinary thirteen-year-old kid from London. No. Not me.*

But the man just laughed. "You've been out in the sun too long, my boy. The heat has broiled your brain. Shade is what you need. Now come inside. Really. I do insist."

Tim hated it when grown-ups referred to him that way. "I'm not your boy," he shouted. He kicked some dirt and then some bones at the man for good measure. "And I'm not going into your . . . that place, whatever it is. I didn't mean to come here. And I don't mean to stay here."

The man tsk-tsked and touched his long fingers to the middle of his forehead as if he were thinking deep thoughts. "Let me guess. You set out for Faerie. Only you found yourself here. And as a result, you are disappointed and hence disagreeable." The man raised his eyebrows as if he were expecting Tim to confirm this theory.

"Well, child. This *is* Faerie." The man held out his arms in an expansive gesture. "All of it that matters, at any rate. All that's real. Beyond those walls"—he pointed the riding crop at the wall that Tim had just fallen from—"all is illusion. Consider yourself fortunate to have found this place. An oasis of rationality in the midst of a desert of superstition." He tucked the riding crop under his arm.

Tim narrowed his eyes. This place looked nothing like Faerie. Then he remembered the desert wasteland Tamlin had brought him to. He hadn't believed that desolate landscape was Faerie either. This man might actually be telling the truth.

"Now we must enter your name in the master register," the man said. "What did you say your name was?"

Tim sneered. Did this bloke think he was as dumb as all that? He wasn't going to fall for the oldest trick in the book. Tim kicked a large femur toward the man. "Bone," Tim replied. "Jack Bone. And you?"

"Ahh. You are a clever boy, aren't you?"

Tim noticed the man's smile was tight with anger. He also realized there was something seriously wrong with the guy's mouth. The man took a step closer.

Tim's nose wrinkled. *What a stink. This freak could use extra-strength mouthwash.* His breath had the foul odor of old blood and bad meat.

"As much as I appreciate your ready wit, I hate an impasse," the man said. "A tie, as it were. Perhaps if I am more direct, we can come to terms more quickly." He placed his fingertips together lightly and formed a little triangle of his hands. He licked his lips. "I propose a game."

"A game," Tim repeated. He didn't like the sound of that. He also knew he had no idea how to escape from this place, so he had to hear the guy out.

"Yes. And to make the game more interesting, what shall we play for? What are the stakes?" A slow smile tried to make its way across the man's face, but it was as if his lips were stuck. They only made it partway into a smile.

"Ahhh. I know. I know what should tempt a clever boy. I can tell you who your father is."

Tim felt little prickles under his hair. How

could this man know that was the reason Tim had come to Faerie? *Can he read my mind?*

"Yes, I will tell you about your father, child, if you can best me at my game."

Tim narrowed his eyes. "I don't believe you."

"No? But it is a question you'd love to learn the answer to, you don't deny."

Tim swallowed hard. He couldn't come up with a clever retort or a decent bluff.

"And consider this," the man continued. "How could I know the question if I did not know the answer?"

Tim had to admit that there was some sort of twisted logic there. "What if I lose?" he asked.

"If you lose, you'll accept my tutelage. You will become my student. I will liberate you from all of your illusions."

Tim gazed around at the courtyard, at the decaying and brittle bones. He put the evidence together with the unmistakable odor emanating from the man. "And then you'll eat me."

The man didn't seem to care that Tim had figured this out. "Eventually, yes," he said casually. "But you won't care when that time comes. You won't care at all." The man cracked his knuckles.

Jeez, Tim thought, *he's the type who probably enjoys scratching his fingernails on a chalkboard.*

"You see, I'll consume your magic before I

touch your flesh. You might be surprised to learn how little one cares for one's flesh once one's soul has been stripped away."

Tim swallowed hard, to keep the sick bile he felt in his stomach from rising. What kind of monster was he facing?

The man knelt down and picked up two small skeletons. Tim thought they might have once been flitlings, the pretty, graceful creatures he had seen at the Queen's palace. Handling them with surprising delicacy, the man fashioned the bones so that they were able to stand in the dirt, posing them like macabre action figures. Figures without flesh. Just bones.

Tim glanced over at the wall again. Then at the mansion. Then at the man. What choice did he have? "Okay," he agreed.

Besides, he thought, *maybe I can actually win*. He would do his best, at any rate.

The man stood back up. "Bravo," he said. He clapped his hands so lightly they made no sound. "I'm so pleased that we could settle our differences in so civilized a manner. Now we have world enough and time to know each other better, as the poet said."

Tim cringed as the man clapped a hand on his shoulder. Tim tried shaking it off, but his grip was too strong.

"I would like to tell you the axiom that rules my life." The man guided Tim toward the ominous mansion. "It is the center of all that I do. *Fronti nulla fides*, delectable boy." He passed his arm in front of his face, covering his mouth, and rubbed his fingers over his lips as if he was in deep thought. He lowered his hand and Tim gasped. The man had three daggerlike sets of teeth in his mouth.

"In appearances place no faith," the man declared.

What is he? Tim wondered. He stared at the set of teeth that went from ear to ear, as if the man's jaws could unhinge and open wide enough to swallow Tim whole. In the center, where a human's mouth usually was, were another two sets of teeth, one immediately behind the other. And all the teeth looked razor sharp.

The man strolled toward the crumbling mansion, dragging Tim with him. "As you shall see, I have a vocation," he explained, "a most singular and satisfying goal. I am simplifying the world."

They had arrived at the threshold of the enormous house. Tim's heart was pounding hard, but he knew there was no turning back. Old Toothy would make certain of that. Tim's only hope of survival was beating the creature somehow.

The door opened and Tim stepped inside,

hearing the man lock the door behind him. The first thing that hit Tim was the smell of death and of something chemical. It reminded him of his school's science lab.

Tim stood in a dark, cavernous hallway. It took a minute for his eyes to adjust to the light. When they did, his mouth dropped open. In front of him were rows of glass cases, like in a museum, each housing an amazing animal. There were also creatures stuffed and sitting on pedestals, others pinned to display boards. Each had an identifying card, listing its specimen number.

"They're all . . . they're all dead," Tim said.

"Are they?" the man asked. "How can you say a creature is dead when it can't be proved that it ever lived?"

Tim whirled and glared at the horrible man. "Why did you do this to them?" he demanded.

The man wasn't fazed at all. In fact, he seemed to enjoy Tim's outburst. "Ahh, how refreshing," he said. "An eager student. I am going to enjoy you, child. It is such a pleasure to cleanse young minds of the taint of credulity. But as for your question, I've already answered it. I am engaged in simplifying the world. In time, you will comprehend the—"

"Shut up!" Tim cried, cutting off the man's words. "Just shut up!"

"Pardon?" Tim heard a sharp edge in the man's voice, but he didn't care. He just wanted the man to stop speaking for a minute. He needed to think.

Tim slowly turned to face his hideous adversary. "I've changed my mind," he announced, "about your game."

The man brought his face a mere few inches from Tim. "You've agreed to the game, little man." Tim could hear threat in every syllable. "You cannot decline to play now."

"I'm not backing out," Tim told him. "I just want to change the terms of the bet."

The man straightened back up and crossed his arms, waiting. He looked suspicious. *Fine. Let him worry for a change.*

"I don't want you tell me my father's name after I've beaten you," Tim said, mustering all his courage and bluster. "It's *your* name I want to know." *And once I have it*, Tim thought, *I shall destroy you.*

"Ah, such fire. Anger becomes you, child." The man cocked his head to one side. "I can be generous. If you can indeed beat me at my game, you shall have *both* names! Mine and your father's. You will have earned them, I'm sure. I've become quite adept at hide and seek, you see."

The man smiled, and Tim had to look away

from that grotesque mouth.

The man turned and headed toward a heavy double door. He gripped the handles, then glanced back over his shoulder at Tim. "I will be with you presently. If you need me for anything I will be in the conservatory, playing my flute."

The man stepped through the doorway, and the doors slowly swung shut.

Tim sank to the bottom step of the sweeping stairway. He buried his face in his hands, finally allowing himself to feel all the fear that had been building since the creature first appeared.

"Oh man," he moaned. "What have I done?"

Tamlin circled over Faerie. He saw another dead place. Another legend swallowed up by the wasteland. *Is this Arraune, where the lake women wove water and sighs into blue-green silk? Or is this Tellis, where lost hopes paced the streets, begging strangers to take them in? I cannot tell. Something has eaten the heart of this place. The life of it is gone.*

In his sad, wearisome journey, Tamlin could see that the lands were wearing away everywhere. Fading. *Faerie is less than a ghost of what she was when her gates were first opened to me*, he observed.

Tamlin thought back to the time before he had become an inhabitant of Faerie. It was so long ago, centuries. He had not been more than twenty summers old but he had already stolen droves of cattle from neighbors not of his clan. He had murdered a distant cousin who had made light of his sister's chastity. His kinsmen sang of his courage. *A knight, they reckoned me,* he thought. *But I was a coward. I know that now.*

Tamlin continued his flight, but now he saw only his past, not the withering land below him. *I believed in nothing and in no one. Myself, least of all. I was a raw and arrogant whelp, and I might have grown into a cur. But I was given a glimpse of mystery. A mystery as precious as life itself. Faerie.*

Tamlin recalled meeting Titania that fateful night in the moonlight. Why she had entered his world he still did not know. But once she did, his life was changed forever. For it was she who had brought him here. To Faerie. And while he had been a prisoner, it was only in later years that he became a reluctant one. And even then, while he strained against Titania's whims and tempers, Faerie herself had always rewarded him.

The twilight land dared me to have faith in my own madness, he acknowledged. *To embrace what I had hidden from myself all my wretched and cautious life: the world around me and the world within me. The land taught me to live. To laugh. And, yes, even to love.*

Now the Summerland was dead. It had been strangled and sucked dry. *This wasteland spills from the soul of Faerie's murderer.* Tamlin was determined to find the evil source of such devastation. And then? *Whoever makes this cruel magic can consume dreams easily enough, it seems. We'll see how he fares against one whose dreams vanished long ago.*

One thought comforted Tamlin, as he flew in low circles searching for his enemy. *At least I did not bring the boy into this hell, to face this battle. How surprising to have Amadan to thank for anything, but I do have to thank him for this. If the insidious flitling had not interrupted me, I would have brought the boy here, and that I would regret now. Barren of dreams his world might be, but at least he is safe now.*

Chapter Nine

WHAT KIND OF LOON WOULD *build a house like this?* Tim had just come to another dead end, another hallway that led to nowhere. Just a blank wall. He turned around and found his way back to the main passageway. The soft, embroidered carpet under his feet and the rows of chandeliers overhead did nothing to disguise the fact that this house was a trap. Plain and simple.

Tim was reminded of another biology question. They had just had this on an exam from their unit on animal behavior. The question was: Not all carnivores are _____, but all _____ are carnivores. It had been his task to fill in the blanks and it had been easy. The answer was *predators*.

Predators don't just kill their prey and eat it, Tim remembered. *That would be too easy. Predators enjoy tracking and stalking their meals. It's all a big game to the predator. A game. That was precisely what this bloke had suggested.* And Tim believed without any doubt that this house was a predator's dream palace.

None of the doors had a lock to hide behind. No knives handy in the kitchen with which to defend oneself. *Not that I've found a kitchen. In fact*, Tim realized as he wandered the broad hallways, poking his head through archways, *this freak probably eats all his meals raw.*

Tim found himself at the front door again. He scratched his head. The house was a maze, with rooms leading into halls back into rooms. They all twisted and opened out where you didn't expect them to. He wasn't even certain how he had ended up back where he had started. Tim stood with his hands on his hips, trying to get his bearings.

Off to his left, through the heavy double doors, Tim could hear the lilting sound of a flute. The creep hadn't been kidding. He really was a music lover. He didn't even sound half bad. *Phenomenal, considering all those teeth*. Tim wouldn't have picked a wind instrument for someone with a mouth like that.

In front of him, the room opened out into the sicko display area, filled with glass cases and pedestals and sad stuffed creatures. Tim tried not to look any of them in the eye. The ceiling was quite high in that area, and little balconies ran along both sides. *The spiral staircase at the far end of the room must provide access to that mezzanine,* Tim figured.

To the right was the broad, sweeping marble staircase leading to the upper floors. Tim wished he had paid more attention outside to the layout of the house. He remembered turrets with windows in them, and—

Windows! He might be able to use that stone Tamlin had given him to smash through the glass and make an escape! So it might just land him back in the courtyard with the ever-growing wall, but he'd rather be outside than trapped in here.

Tim had already tried wishing himself out with the stone, but nothing had happened. The amulet didn't even look the same inside this horrible house. It had lost its luster and sheen and looked just like an ordinary rock. It was as if the mansion—or that man—had dulled the stone's magic.

But a rock is still a rock. Tim dashed to the brocade drapes that blocked out the light. He yanked them aside.

His shoulders sagged. The windows were barred, and they had what looked like steel mesh built right into them.

"That was dumb," Tim admonished himself. "This guy has been at this game for years—centuries even. Did you really think it would be as simple as that?"

Frustration flooded through him. He stalked away from the windows, his hands clenched in tight fists. As he walked through the archway he slammed his fist into the doorframe.

Crrreeeeaak.

Tim's eyes widened in surprise as he saw the wood paneling open in the wall beside the archway. He stared at his fist and then at the dark opening. A secret passageway. *And it looks too small for that creep to crawl into. Excellent!*

Tim hoisted himself up into the little doorway and pulled the door shut behind him. Dust flew everywhere, and he coughed into his sleeve, trying to mask the sound. Now that he had found a place to hide, he didn't want to give it away just because of massive dust bunnies!

Tim's eyes adjusted to the dimness of the cramped space, and he saw that it was actually the start of a tunnel. It branched off in all different directions. He began to crawl, wanting to put distance between him and the opening. *Even if he couldn't fit comfortably in here*, Tim acknowledged, *that guy must know this secret passageway exists.*

Tim came to the first branch, and his heart sank. It opened right into the large main room. No secret door to protect him; the opening wasn't even hidden behind a display case. Tim peered out exactly at the freak's eye level. If the man was standing anywhere in that room he'd see Tim right this minute. Tim snorted. *Yeah, this was a big secret.*

Maybe somewhere deeper in, he thought, crawling again. He arrived at a turn in the tunnel and found a flight of stairs. Here he could almost stand, so he took the steps in a low crouch. It twisted and turned so many times Tim had no idea if he was at the front or back of the house. It didn't matter where he was, as long as Toothy didn't find him.

He came to a landing and leaned against the wall, trying to get his bearings. "Ooops!" He fell backward through a doorway and landed hard on his backside. "Ow," he complained. He sat back up and crossed his legs. *That wasn't even a wall*, he realized. *It was just canvas painted to look like it was. Sneaky.*

There are all sorts of places for you to hide, Tim observed as he began crawling again. *And all sorts of ways for someone to sneak up on you while you're hiding*.

Tim found a room that looked promising. It was filled with nooks and crannies and junk like trunks and mounds of fabric. He might be able to hide in a trunk or cover himself with one of the drapes and pretend to be part of the furniture.

Tim crossed quickly to the trunk. He was reaching to open it when the back of his neck prickled. Something was wrong. He glanced behind him and gulped. A row of sharp knives stuck out of the wall behind him, the razor-sharp tips pointing straight out. Tim was in the direct line of fire.

He looked down at the trunk again. "I bet if I . . ." he murmured. On a hunch, he moved away from the trunk. He found a poker by the enormous fireplace. Gripping it, he lay on the floor as far away from the trunk as he could get and still reach it with the poker. He held the poker in two hands and lifted the trunk lid with it.

Thwick! Thwick! Thwick!

The knives flew across the room. Without Tim's body to stop them, they flung themselves into the tapestry hanging on the opposite wall.

The poker clattered to the floor. The trunk had been rigged. If Tim had opened it from the front, he'd be a pincushion right now. He could feel sweat bead up on his forehead. He had to be more careful—every single room could have a booby trap in it, a deadly one.

He pushed himself up to sit, then sank back onto his heels. "All kinds of rooms and halls and ups and downs that look like places you'd be safe," he muttered, "until you get inside them and you discover that they're traps."

He felt exhausted. How could he possibly survive this game? What else lay out there waiting to impale him, suffocate him, or hold him prisoner until that man showed up? He took a deep breath and shook his head. "Don't think about that," he told himself. "Staying alive. That's what you want to think about right now."

He stood and crossed to the knives embedded in the tapestry to their hilts. Did he dare touch them? Try to use one as a weapon? For all he knew they were coated with poison. Deciding to risk it, he wrapped his fingers around the carved black handle of the knife in front of him and tugged.

The knife didn't budge. He tried again. The same thing happened. It was as if the knife were now stuck in hardened cement.

"Well, you're no help," he told the wall of knives. *Keep playing the game*, Tim reminded himself. *If you concentrate on keeping yourself in one piece, everything else will take care of itself. At least*, he thought, *that's how it works in fairy tales.*

Tim went back to trying to find a hiding place, or at least a way to keep himself one step ahead of his predatory host. He noticed that the flute playing had stopped. Tim wasn't certain if that was because he was now out of hearing range or because the man had started hunting for him.

Fairy tales. Bloody fairy tales. Tim hoisted himself up into a little recess in the wall. As he had expected, it led to another tunnel. This one was very dusty, as if it hadn't been traveled in some time. That struck Tim as a good sign.

Somehow the monsters never seem as real as the princes and princesses do, Tim thought. *The ogres and the giants never seem to have a chance, really. Even the brave little tailors and clever orphan girls make mincemeat out of them. And live happily ever after. That's how they end, the stories.* Now that he was in a real-life fairy tale, complete with its own monster, he realized how unlikely those stories really were.

Probably because they're told by grown-ups. More lies.

Tim spotted daylight at the end of the tunnel he was in. Could it actually be an exit? Since there weren't footprints in the narrow passageway, and there were plenty of cobwebs, this could be a way out that the man had forgotten about. Tim picked up speed, banging his knees and bumping his head as he made his way to the end of the tunnel.

"Whoa!" he exclaimed. The tunnel opened out onto a narrow platform. If Tim had been moving any faster, he would have pitched right over the edge. It was a sheer drop of about thirty feet.

Tim peered down below him and into a courtyard of rubble and bones. On the top of a pile of skeletons lay a young girl—obviously a recent victim. She was still dressed in a beautiful flowing gown and had a tiara on her head. She looked like she might have been a princess—or had been playing dress up. Her body was twisted and broken. Tim couldn't tell if she had been killed by the horrible man or if she had plunged to her death from the very spot he was now in.

Tim was filled with horror and deep sadness for the little girl. He began to choke up. *Maybe she was clever and brave. Maybe she would have done all right, if she'd been in somebody's bedtime story. But she wasn't. And neither am I. So I need to hold myself together.*

This is going from bad to worse to even worse than that. Tim gritted his teeth. He was determined not to let this beastly man get the better of him. "I won't give up!" he declared. His voice echoed around the courtyard. "I just won't! I'll beat you for me, and for that little girl, and for this Land—whether it's Faerie or not!"

Tim tried to calm himself, backed up, and began searching for another place to hide. *Why would these tunnels be built so low?* Tim wondered. *Can Creepy Bloke even fit in here? I wonder if that guy does a lot of crawling around on his hands and knees. I guess he's crazy enough for that.* His mind was rambling to distract him from the horrible sight of the girl.

Or maybe . . . Tim stopped crawling. He froze with one hand off the floor, one knee raised. *Or maybe it's because he doesn't always go around standing up. Maybe he doesn't always have two legs. He could be some sort of animal, when he's at home.*

Tim placed his knee and his hand on the floor. Every muscle ached from his awkward journey through the twists and turns of this bizarre mansion. He was still being pursued and he still had no place to hide.

A new thought occurred to Tim. Perhaps hiding wasn't really the way to go. *The other ones—the previous victims,* he reasoned, *it looks as if they all tried to hide and look where it got them.*

But he had to do something. He couldn't just wait around to be turned into snack food. But what?

Tim crawled out of an archway into another long hallway with a marble floor and several closed doors.

He stood up and carefully tried the first door he came to. It was locked. Surprised, he tried the ornate door handle again. In all of his exploring he had yet to find a single door that had been locked. Until now.

Now that's interesting. . . .

Chapter Ten

IF THIS DOOR WAS LOCKED, then it was pretty obvious that the master of the house did not want anyone to go into that room—which made it precisely the place Tim wanted to be.

But how could he get in? Tim shoved his hands into his pockets as he thought about this. He felt the stone that Tamlin had given him. It hadn't worked before and he didn't think it would work now. Not in its present, dull state.

The fingers of his other hand wrapped around something hard. He pulled it out of his pocket.

Tim stared down at an old-fashioned key. His brow furrowed. He had completely forgotten that he had brought it with him.

This key had nearly cost him his freedom—perhaps now it would save him.

He hoped it would work. He didn't think another world lay behind that door—just safety or information. He stepped up to the door and slid the heavy key into the lock, hoping fervently that this plan would work. He heard a satisfying click, and the door swung open.

Tim was in an enormous library. There were more books in this room than Tim had ever seen in a single place in his life. More than at school, more than at the bookshop. Even more than at the library three streets over from Molly's place. He put the key back in his pocket and took a step deeper inside.

The bookshelves rose from the floor to the ceiling, and there were rows and rows of them. Most of the books looked dusty and old, but there were some newer ones, too.

Tim walked around the first bookcase, hoping to get a sense of the size of the room. Along the wall were more of those horrible display cases. This time, Tim forced himself to look. He knew his life depended on figuring out everything he could about how Toothy operated.

The first case held a large beast, some sort of cross between a lion and an eagle. The display card hanging beside it read GRIFFIN. SPECIMEN NUMBER 21. Tim walked a little farther along the wall and came to a pedestal with an animal that also seemed to be part lion. Only this one had the head of a woman. He recognized it from ancient civilization in history class. It was a sphinx. He remembered learning that the giant sphinx that still stood in Egypt was a large version of thousands of little statues of these creatures that were found all over Egypt.

Maybe they had so many statues of them because they once were real, Tim thought. *And they're all gone now, maybe thanks to this guy's extermination plan. What had he called it? Oh yeah.* "'Simplifying the world,'" Tim murmured.

He came to a low platform. There was nothing on it. "That's weird." He glanced at the label on the wall and his heart did a flip-flop. FAIR FOLK, it said.

So far, Tim hadn't seen anything set up to display humans. "Well, duh," Tim scoffed at himself. "You don't display your meals."

Tim peered down a row of bookshelves and realized there was a large open space in the center of the library that he hadn't seen before. Curious, he moved to where he could see more clearly.

"Oh no," he gasped.

An extraordinary creature stood on a pedestal in the center of the room.

"You're so beautiful," Tim whispered. "And he got you, too."

A unicorn stood before him, silent and

motionless, surrounded by the phalanx of book-shelves. Tim knew it was no longer alive, but he had to move closer. He wanted to touch it, pet it, stroke its white mane. He didn't care if that was silly. The unicorn was so magnificent it simply drew Tim toward it.

As he moved toward the unicorn, he realized he had stepped onto a crumpled piece of paper. Bending down, he saw that it was a page that had been torn from a book.

He gazed down at the piece of paper in his hands. On it was printed an illustration of a uni-corn with a description of it underneath. The writing looked old-fashioned, and there were Latin words scattered throughout the paragraph.

Then he noticed that a book was pulled part-way out from the bottom bookshelf, its binding sticking out a few inches. "*Terra Incognita*," Tim read. He sat down cross-legged on the floor, picked up the book, and flipped it open.

"What the—?" Page after page had been torn from the book. He glanced at the unicorn page. It had obviously been torn from this very book. But why? Why would anyone rip out all the pages of a book? And then why would he put it back on the shelf?

Not all the pages have been torn out, Tim real-ized. "Ugh. That dude sure is ugly." He stared down at the picture on the only remaining page in the volume.

"Manticore," Tim read. *Hm. Never heard of one of those.* The creature was another one of those mixed-up half-this, half-that beasts. But it wasn't elegant and mysterious like the sphinx. The manticore was just gross. And mean-looking. It had a lion's body, except its tail looked like a scorpion's. It also had the face of a man, but what a face! Its eyes looked crazed, and it had a mouth with rows of teeth.

Tim particularly noted the part that explained it had an appetite for humans.

"Harrum." Tim heard behind him.

He started, and dropped the book. *Sheesh. Does the guy have allergies or something? Or is that throat clearing a nervous tick?* He picked the book back up, closed it, and lay it across his knees. He chose not to get up, trying to act like he didn't care that the guy had just snuck up on him.

"How did you get in here?" the man demanded.

"I have my ways," Tim retorted. "I'm not just a dumb kid, you know." He lay the crinkled unicorn page on the book and smoothed the paper.

"I see that you've already begun your studies," the man commented.

"I'm looking at this book, that's all." He lifted

up the book for the man to see. "Why do you even bother to pretend it's a book at all when you've torn out all the pages? That's stupid."

"I do not *pretend* that this is a book, insolent child," the man snapped. "This *is* a book."

Tim glanced over his shoulder up at the man. The man fussed with his long hair as if he were collecting himself. "I have, in the interests of scholarship," he said, much more calmly, "removed from the volume certain entries that I determined to be extraneous, as they dealt with creatures whose existence my researches have disproved."

Now Tim couldn't contain his anger. He leaped to his feet, letting the book thud to the floor. He waved the unicorn page at the creep. "Like the unicorn, you mean? You're lying. It's a lot realer than that ugly *thing* in your stupid book. The only page you left in it."

"You wound me, boy," the man said. "Voicing this claptrap, you dash my expectations." He waved toward the display cases along the wall. "Oh, the creatures I've subtracted from my bestiaries may have served a purpose once," he said loftily. He pointed at the unicorn on the pedestal behind Timothy. "The unicorn, for example, that you seem to have fixated on. Certainly, the unicorn was a staple of the ballads with which troubadours entertained many a milkmaid. A pretty concept, that is all." He stepped up so closely to Tim the boy could smell the man's foul breath. "But it is nothing," the man hissed.

Tim backed up a few steps from the stench. "Don't tell me you don't believe in magic," Tim scoffed.

"I believe in food," the man declared. "And I believe in myself." He crossed his arms over his chest, his eyes narrowing. "But we will discuss this later."

Tim thought the man sounded peeved. *Fine. It's not like we were going to be friends, and it isn't as if getting the guy mad puts me in any greater danger.* He knew he had been in danger since the moment he landed in the bone-filled courtyard.

"I sought you out with conversation in mind," the man fretted. "But I find myself no longer in the mood to chitchat. You've put me out of sorts, you see. So I am going away for the briefest moment possible, my dumpling. And I am going to change into something a bit more comfortable."

A nasty smile spread across the man's face. With all those teeth, the expression was grotesque.

Tim's heart thudded. *That smile. Those teeth!*

"When I return, we shall finish our game, once and for all." The man turned to go.

It has to be—! Tim flipped open the book again and ripped out the last remaining page. *The manticore!*

"Wait," Tim called, holding the torn page behind his back. "I'm sorry. Really. I didn't mean to insult you." The man slowly turned around. "Didn't you?" He sounded skeptical.

Since this creepo kept referring to Tim as an "eager student," Tim figured he should go all wide-eyed and humble.

"I just meant that I didn't understand what you said about the unicorn." He jerked his head toward the unicorn on the pedestal. "I mean, it looks sort of real. Sort of three-dimensional even if it is a bit tatty." He gazed down at the floor and made a small circle with his toes. "I've never been very bright. I know."

The man took a step closer. "Do tell."

Tim played up the pathetic act big-time. "I failed biology twice." He hadn't really, but biology was a subject that had seemed to come up a lot lately. "But please, sir—if you'd try to explain about the unicorn. In little words so I can understand. I'm sure you're a better teacher than my old one back home ever was, or could ever hope to be."

The man clapped his hands together with delight. "Enough, my cherub. Say no more." He chucked Tim under the chin. Tim forced himself not to cringe. "No doubt your education has been deficient, if not defective. But you must not reproach yourself on that score. You have never had a teacher deserving of the name until this moment. Come, my cupcake. And I'll explain the unicorn."

The man put his arm around Tim and walked him to the pedestal where the unicorn stood, motionless and unseeing.

"It is remarkable, I must say, that this is the specimen that captured your imagination," the man declared, "since it was, in a sense, the unicorn who made me what I am today."

"Really." Tim tried not to gag from the man's foul smell, not to mention those multiple teeth.

"Indeed, my poppet. Had I never encountered the beast, I might never have discovered my purpose or my power."

Tim could tell he was in for a long story, sort of like when he visited Auntie Blodwyn in Brighton and his uncles all felt compelled to talk of their war years. On and on for hours. Well, as long as the guy kept talking, Tim would stay alive. And have the chance to come up with a plan.

"I had simple appetites in the old days," the man said. "One can consume no end of flesh, you see, and still be racked by hunger." He said this as if he were confiding some great secret to Tim.

Words of wisdom, as it were. "One's soul is ever so much more difficult to fill than one's belly. I was a tragic figure in those days. Unfulfilled, ravenous for I knew not what. Until this shabby creature wandered into my life."

He gestured at the unicorn with a flourish, like the ringmaster of a circus introducing an act. Tim was able to casually slip out of the man's grip. He couldn't stand the feel of the guy's fingers on him.

"I should not fault you for believing in the unicorn," the man continued. "When I first spied the brute, I myself was almost persuaded of its reality."

The man walked slowly all around the unicorn's pedestal, gazing up at it, as if he were reliving the very first time he had ever seen it. "Its silver hide shimmered in the half light, and its spiral horn glittered. It was only upon closer inspection that I was able to perceive the details which led me to understand that no beast so splendid could live. Did I say live?" Now his eyes bored into Tim's. "I meant to say *exist*."

Why? Tim wondered silently. *Why can't beauty and wonder be part of the world?*

The man looked up at the unicorn again, completing his circuit around it. "I realized that the shimmer of its hide derived solely from a coating of silica dust." He poked the unicorn's side with his riding crop. Tim flinched. "The poor brute must have spent half its life rolling on sandy riverbanks. To rid itself of vermin, I conjecture. Filthy thing."

He stood beside Tim again. Tim hoped he wouldn't get much closer. The odor emanating from the man was awful, and Tim had the worrisome idea that the guy could smell his fear. Most predators could do that.

"I developed a theory—the myth of the unicorn had its beginning in a fascinating interplay of human gullibility and greed. It goes like this. Once upon a time, a very clever man fastened a goat's horn to a horse and exhibited the beast at taverns and country fairs. He did this with the sole aim of bilking ale-addled farmers of their hard-earned coppers. The unicorns of legend were all simply variations of this clever man's scheme."

The man smiled with smug satisfaction. Tim wanted to smack him.

"Now that I had such a beast frolicking in my courtyard, I could test this theory. Fortunately, the unicorn expired. Perhaps the ambiance of my garden disagreed with it."

No joke, Tim thought, remembering the piles of scattered bones in the courtyard. *This creep has been eating flesh all of his life. That had to be a turnoff to an animal as glorious as a unicorn.*

"I dissected the beast. When my researches were done, I could prove without a doubt that the myths were wrong. Then I preserved the specimen. And thus began my collection."

The man stepped up onto the platform with the unicorn. He sneered with his horrible tooth-filled smile. "The eyes are beautiful, are they not?" He flicked one with his long fingers. It made a little pinging sound. "They're glass, don't you know."

"Stop! Just stop!" Tim shouted. He leaped up onto the platform and flung his arms around the unicorn's neck. He didn't care what the man thought of him, how stupid he might seem. He just didn't care.

"I can't listen to you anymore," Tim said, "not even to stay alive another five minutes. It's not worth it. I'm not going to hide from you, so go do whatever it is you do. Just be quiet about it. You're a liar and a freak and you stink like rotten meat. You think you're some bloody genius. But you're really nothing. Nothing!"

Tim clung to the unicorn, his back to the man, not knowing what would happen next.

There was a long pause. Tim's body shook with a mixture of rage and fear. Any moment, he knew, the man's triple set of teeth could bite down on his neck.

But it didn't happen.

"What an alluring habit you have of wearing

your heart on your sleeve, my little onion," the man said. "It's too tender for words. Very well. I'll see you soon."

Tim waited as he heard the man's footsteps grow more and more distant. The door slammed shut, and Tim was alone in the library.

Well, not exactly alone.

"Maybe he'll exhibit us together," Tim said to the unicorn. "When he's through eating my soul and all. You have to admit, it would make sense." Tim jumped down and stood in front of the pedestal. "And on your left, ladies and gentlemen," he announced in a carnival barker's booming style, "next to the dogs with wings, we have the dumb unicorn and the dumber kid."

Tim gave a shaky laugh, then sank down onto the pedestal. He settled himself between the unicorn's forelegs and pulled his knees up to his chest. "All right. So it is a lame place to hide," he said. "It's as good a place as any to wait, though." He glanced up at the unicorn's face. "You don't mind being talked to, do you? It's just that I don't want my last words to be, 'Well, Tim, that was stupid, wasn't it?' Which is exactly what they'll be if I start talking to *myself*."

Tim rested his chin on his knee. "I don't think you can hide from him, really. Though I'm sure it must make him very happy when you try. Well, I

don't want to give him anything to smile about."
Tim shuddered. "I hate it when he smiles. One set
of teeth should be enough for anybody."

Those teeth. Tim held up the page he had torn
from the man's book, the last remaining page.
*That's what he really is, isn't it? The teeth were the
dead giveaway. A manticore. Or is it* the *manticore?
Maybe there's only one.*

He stared at the page. *Think, Tim*, he admonished himself. *A proper magician wouldn't just sit
here. A proper magician would do something.*

Still, all he could do was stare at the page.
Okay, Tim thought, trying to work it out, *come up
with a plan.* "My friend John Constantine would
probably make a trap out of an empty cigarette
pack or something," he explained to the unicorn.
"Zatanna would talk backward, saying something
like 'Erocitnam, teg deffuts.' Then there's Tamlin,
this guy who might be my father. He says that
magic answers need and that power is in little
things."

He craned his neck around to look at the unicorn's face. "So, unicorn, what would be a little
thing that could help me tap into magic and get
me out of this place?"

Tim turned back around and held up the picture of the manticore. He squinted at it, as if a
new angle would help him come up with an idea.

"I could try sticking pins into this or setting it on fire. But I think I'd have to know his name to make that work. Or would it be enough to know *what* he is?"

I suppose I could try anyway. "Just one problem," he told the unicorn. "I don't have any pins or matches."

"Pins? Matches? You'd work a death spell on me on the sly? And I thought we had come to an understanding."

Startled, Tim looked up. He had never heard the man come in. Only he wasn't a man anymore. A huge, full-size, larger-than-life manticore stood in front of him. It was as if the illustration in his hands had come to life—only enlarged by a thousand percent.

The man's head had not changed—same greasy red hair, same grotesque mouth, same triple set of teeth. Only now that head sat atop a lion's massive body.

Before Tim could make a move, the manticore leaped upon him, grabbing his ankle in its paws and yanking him from the pedestal. The sheet of paper went flying and Tim landed hard on the floor.

"Let me go!" Tim cried. He kicked out hard and balled his hands into fists, hitting whatever he could. He wriggled, trying to keep the manticore from getting a good shot at biting his throat.

None of this seemed to faze the manticore. He still spoke calmly. "Go? Oh, no, I think not." The manticore sat on Tim, nearly crushing the air out of him. Its scorpion tail flicked, and its teeth dripped with greenish-yellow venom.

"I had intended to take the time to educate you. To play Socrates to your Plato before I ate you. But, alas, you've changed my mind."

Tim pushed as hard as he could up against the beast, trying to get him off his chest. The manticore pinned his arms back with its massive paws.

"Cease your struggling," the manticore ordered.

Tim's efforts made him sweaty—and his wrist slipped out from under one of the manticore's heavy paws. He used his free hand to punch the beast hard on the nose.

The manticore reared up with a roar, allowing Tim to wiggle a bit further out from under him, before it slammed back down on top of him, slashing Tim's arm as it pinned him back on the floor. Tim was astonished by the sight of his own blood spurting out, spattering across the torn pages of the book that lay scattered on the ground around them.

"Ohhh, it hurts," Tim moaned. He tried to roll up into a little ball, but the manticore held him down.

"I told you to stop your struggling, did I not?"

"Manticore," Tim declared, as the world spun around him. "I know who you are. But I know something else, too. I don't care what you think—that unicorn is real!"

Tim heard a loud whinny. He watched, amazed, as the unicorn underwent an extraordinary transformation. The creature's pure white coat glowed, as if it were lit from within. Each clearly defined muscle rippled, shuddering back into life. The unicorn lifted its head and blinked its once-glass eyes. Tim had done it! Magic *had* answered a need. And Tim used that magic to bring the unicorn back to life.

The manticore's human head whirled around. "What?" he cried. "No! How can it be?"

The unicorn reared up. A crackling energy shot through the room again. Sparks flew from its single horn. As its two front feet rose in the air, Tim saw that the manticore page had stuck to one of the unicorn's hooves. *My blood*, Tim realized. *That's what's making it stick.*

The unicorn crashed down. Using its horn, it ripped the manticore page from its hoof, then speared the beast itself—right through its heart.

"Agghhhhhhh!" The manticore howled in agony. He rolled off Tim, and collapsed beside him.

Chapter Eleven

ON AND ON TAMLIN FLEW, uncertain of how to find his quarry, the maker of this nightmare. But then everything began to change.

Tamlin circled over the land, astonished. He watched flowers bursting out of rocks, rivers suddenly overflowing their beds. It was as if a black-and-white picture were being colored in with sparkling paints.

"Who could have hoped for this?" he exclaimed. "The land becomes herself again! How did this happen?" Now Tamlin had a new goal—to discover the great magician who could have worked this miracle, who could have broken the bindings that Titania herself could not undo.

From his vantage point high above the ground, Tamlin could pinpoint the center of the bountiful magic. The miraculous changes flowed out from one spot.

* * *

Tim was thirsty. So thirsty. He didn't think he'd ever been so thirsty in all of his life. Not during gym class. Not after a heavy session of skateboarding. Not even in the middle of summer.

Something nudged him. He opened his eyes slowly and squinted up at a pure white unicorn peering down at him. The beautiful creature had gently prodded Tim with its horn.

"Oh, it's you," Tim said. "Would it be okay with you if I lie here for a bit? Just until things stop spinning. Thanks."

Wait a sec. Aren't I supposed to be terrified right now? Aren't I in mortal combat with an evil creature? Oh yeah . . . It began to come back.

"Hey, where's the manticore?" Tim asked the unicorn. "He was just—oooww," Tim moaned as he pushed himself up to a sitting position. It was then he spotted the manticore. Only it wasn't exactly the manticore anymore. It had turned into a manticore-shaped sand pile.

"Oh, there he is," Tim murmured. He looked at the unicorn. "How did you do that? Not that I'm complaining, mind you." Tim leaned over the pile of manticore dust.

"Hah! He got you," Tim taunted the creature. "Or maybe *we* got you. Whatever. Serves you right, Socrates."

Tim slowly and shakily rose to his feet. He had to lean against the unicorn's side to steady himself. He clutched his still-bleeding arm and gazed around him.

The courtyard was no longer filled with bones. It was bursting with flowers. The stench had lifted, and fragrant scents wafted on a sweet breeze. The ever-growing wall suddenly had a doorway in it, and Tim and the unicorn made their way through to the other side.

"Look at that," Tim whispered. Rolling green hills lay before him. As weak as he was, Tim couldn't stop himself from venturing into the tall grasses, to marvel at the astonishing sight. So the manticore hadn't been lying. Tim really was in Faerie, and now the realm was being restored all around him.

"Cool!" Tim exclaimed.

Then, suddenly, he felt the little energy he had leave him, and he collapsed.

Tamlin beat his strong wings and quickly made his way to the source. His heart leaped into his mouth.

It was the boy. And the child was not alone. He was being guarded by that most pure creature, a unicorn.

What is Tim doing here? Tamlin wondered.

How did he get here? The answer came to him in a rush of clarity. *I gave him the Opening Stone, and he opened a way for himself into this world. I should have known. The prophecies* are *true. My child lives, and he is full of magic.*

Tamlin landed and transformed into man shape. The unicorn tipped its horn in greeting, then galloped away.

Tamlin kneeled down beside the boy. "Timothy," he said, trying to rouse the child.

"About that Coke," the boy murmured. Tim felt hands—human hands—turn him over gently.

"Tim, you're burning up, child."

Tim gazed up at a face. *I know this face, don't I? Yes. Long straight hair, brown eyes. Cheekbones. What had Tamlin said? Oh, yes.* "No, I'm not burning up. I'm cold. I've been cold for hours."

Tamlin's strong arms cradled Tim, lifting him into an embrace. Then Tamlin leaned Tim against a boulder, propping him upright. That seemed to help his breathing. He lay heavy against the rock, every inhale shallow, every exhale burning.

He wanted to talk and tell Tamlin what he had done, but he didn't have the energy for words. Beating that manticore and then seeing all of Faerie turn back into flowers was brilliant. He was sure Tamlin would think so, too. Tim wanted Tamlin to be proud of him. He couldn't remember why, though.

"We took care of that old manticore," Tim said, when he had enough air to speak. "Me and the unicorn." Why did it hurt so much to talk? So much effort for such a little sound. "At least, I think we did."

"Manticore?" Tamlin repeated. "You've seen the manticore? Here?"

Tim thought Tamlin sounded kind of freaked. Well, the whole thing had been kind of freaky.

"Uh-huh," Tim replied. "He sure is ugly. *Was* ugly, I mean. Before he turned into dust."

"Tim, did it bite you or scratch you or sting you?"

"I guess so. I don't know."

Tim thought Tamlin's voice sounded almost stern. *Maybe I should open my eyes and check out his expression.* Tim's eyelids fluttered. *Nah*, he decided. *Too hard.*

"Hey, there's something I was going to ask you," Tim murmured. "Something important. But I can't remember it just now."

Tim could feel Tamlin's strong hands on him, as if he were searching him for something. He patted Tim's legs, and turned Tim's head first one direction, then another.

"I still have that stone you gave me," Tim

offered. Maybe that's what he was looking for? He didn't want Tamlin to think he'd been careless with it.

Tamlin pulled up Tim's sleeves. "Gods!" Tamlin exclaimed. He gripped Tim's arm in a sore spot. "This scratch is deep and terrible."

"That's okay," Tim assured Tamlin weakly. "It doesn't hurt anymore. Not much."

Tamlin still clutched Tim's arm. "How long ago, child? When did it claw you?"

Tim pulled his arm from Tamlin's grasp and brought his hands up to his face, covering his eyes. The sun was too bright. It hurt, even with his eyes shut. He felt laughter rising, but couldn't quite figure out why. "You know, I just figured it out. I did. I know what holds the world together. Except it's not a what. It's not even an it, really. It's life . . . it's Death."

The piercing light was growing dimmer. The blackness surrounding him was far more comfortable. Out of the black velvet backdrop Tim could make out a shape forming. A familiar shape. "She's pretty. She's very pretty."

A young woman dressed in a black tank top and black jeans, with an ankh pendant dangling from a black ribbon, stood smiling in front of Tim. He remembered her. He had met her at the end of the universe, where he had been taken by the crazy Mr. E.

Well, at least she's not a total stranger, he thought. He finally relaxed and let go . . . into nothingness.

Chapter Twelve

Tim FELT GROGGY AND STIFF. *No wonder*, he realized, *I'm all cramped up on the floor in a corner. A corner of someone's flat.*

He sat upright, immediately on alert. *Now where am I?* He blinked a few times to clear his head and took in his surroundings. *This looks like an ordinary flat*, he noted. But he knew appearances could be deceiving. He shook his head. Where had he just heard that exact phrase? Oh well. He wasn't going to be able to remember. He could tell.

Tim tried to sense for danger, but he was too disoriented to feel much of anything. He leaned against the wall behind him.

A tall, slim young woman with very white skin and blue-black hair stood in front of him. Where did she come from? Had she been there all along? He was seriously out of it.

The woman didn't look much past twenty, and she seemed familiar. Tim worked hard to place her.

"Oh. You," Tim said. "You *are* you, aren't you?" The girl from the end of time. A boy doesn't forget a girl that pretty—particularly when you meet in such a memorable place and in such remarkable circumstances.

The girl smiled. "All the time, and then some," she replied. "Would you like a cup of tea? I've got the kettle on."

A shrill whistle trilled behind a tatty curtain in the doorway. "Oops," the girl said. "There it goes. Come on. If you want good tea, you can't let the water boil too long."

"Really?" Tim had never heard that little bit of wisdom before. Not that he was much of a tea drinker.

"You bet." The girl disappeared behind the curtain. "Really good anything takes timing. Coming?"

Tim climbed to his feet, pushed aside the curtain, and stepped into the main room of the flat. The "kitchen" ran along one wall of the living room—a stove, a fridge, a sink—and the whole place was quite messy. Plates were piled up in the sink, clothes were strewn everywhere. The girl strode to the stove and turned off the gas. The kettle silenced itself.

"This may sound like a silly question, but ummm . . ." Tim's voice trailed off. He knew what he wanted to find out, but he wasn't quite sure how to ask. He was still getting his bearings. He felt all off balance.

The girl rummaged through the cupboards and pulled out a tin of tea. She plopped tea bags into two mugs. Tim wondered if the mugs were clean.

"The only silly questions are the ones you already know the answers to," the girl said. "And it's totally natural to ask those sometimes, too. Ask away."

There was something about this girl's straightforward manner that put Tim at ease. Of all the people he had ever met, she seemed the most comfortable in her own skin. She exuded the same kind of warmth he had felt from Zatanna, the lady magician in California. And Molly, of course. When he let himself feel it.

"Okay, so where—" Tim cut himself off. He didn't really need to know where he was. There was a much more important answer he needed. "What I was really wondering is . . . who are you?"

The girl picked up the kettle and poured boiling water into the two mugs. Steam rose from her mug as she lifted it and took a deep whiff. "Mmmm. Sometimes I brew this stuff just for the smell of it.

Smells more like almonds than almonds do." She handed Tim a mug. "See what I mean?"

"Thank you," he said, taking the mug from her. He took a whiff and pretended to notice the smell. She still hadn't answered his question. *Why is she stalling?*

"You're welcome." She took a sip of tea. "I have a lot of names, Tim. Even if I stuck to my favorites, it would take forever to run through them all. But *who* am I? That's easier to say. I'm Death."

Tim burst out laughing. He couldn't help it. Big hearty, full-out, full-body guffaws. He hoped she didn't get insulted, but he didn't even try to stop himself.

Eventually, Tim's laughter melted down into chuckles. The girl's steady gaze never left him. Then his knees went all wobbly and he sat hard on her sofa.

"Did you say Death? Like with skulls and skeletons and stuff?" He checked her out again. She was dressed all Goth—maybe she was using "Death" as her club name or something. She couldn't really mean she was the Grim Reaper, could she?

"Generally, I have about as much to do with skulls as your average chicken has to do with soufflés. Think about it."

Tim gave her a sideways glance, then blew on his tea to cool it. He took another sip, and images suddenly flooded through him. The manticore. A slashing across his wrist. Burning pain. Blood. Falling. Darkness. Her face.

"Oh," Tim whispered. "I remember now." He carefully placed the mug on the low table in front of him, afraid he would drop it. "You are, aren't you." This time it was a statement, not a question. "That's why you were there at the end of the universe, too."

Death nodded.

Tim went cold. He bent forward and leaned his elbows on his knees. "Will I feel anything?" he asked in a small voice.

"Tim, relax," Death said.

"Easy for you to say," Tim snapped. "You're not the one dying."

"Hey, you can lean on Cavendish, if you want," the girl suggested, "or just hold him. He's good for that."

"Cavendish?" He squinted at her. What was she on about?

"He's right behind you. Wait." She reached behind Tim and handed him a stuffed bear. "He's not the brightest bear in the world, but at least he knows when to keep his mouth shut."

Tim stared at the teddy bear. Was she nuts?

What was he supposed to do with a stupid toy? He didn't want to make her mad though. He figured, since she was Death, if she got angry there would be serious consequences. He sat the teddy bear on his lap.

"Sorry, Tim," she said. "I thought it would take you a while longer to figure it out. You caught on so quickly I didn't have a chance to really prepare you."

She tousled his hair. "That is quite a hearty laugh you have, though. When I told you who I was and you bawled, I almost forgot for a moment that you're a magician."

What did that mean? Tim wondered. *Magicians have no sense of humor? Or did she mean that the life of a magician was so riddled with pain, confusion, and tragedy that there was nothing for a magician to laugh about?* But Tim pushed that thought aside to deal with the present moment.

"So let me see if I've got this right," Tim said slowly. He found he was clutching the teddy bear a little tighter. "I'm dead. Funny. I always thought there'd be more to it."

"You're not dead, trust me." The girl patted Tim's knee. "I'd know if you were. You're pretty close to it though, or I couldn't have brought you here. Not so easily, anyway."

"You brought me here?"

The girl nodded. "Uh-huh. Manticore venom is nasty. Manticores like it that way. If you were in your body right now, you'd be in agony. And when I say agony, I don't mean just pain."

"But—" Tim tried to understand. "You mean you brought me here so I wouldn't suffer? That's bizarre."

The girl looked puzzled. "Why?"

It was so obvious to Tim—why wasn't she getting it? "Well, because you're Death, of course."

"There's nothing bizarre about it," the girl replied. "Death and suffering don't necessarily go together. Hey, do us both a favor, would you?"

"Uh, sure." What favor could she possibly ask of him? He braced himself.

"Don't let that tea get cold." She gave him a grin.

Tim grinned back. She was funny. He liked her, even if she *was* Death.

She seemed to be studying him. "So, you get around a lot," she said, "even for a magician."

Tim put his mug down again. "I wish you'd stop calling me that."

"All right. You get around a lot, period. What are you up to in Faerie?"

"Oh." He fiddled with the teddy bear's foot. "I was just . . . just trying to figure out who my father was. Is. It's sort of . . . sort of . . ." His voice began to break. "Complicated," he finished. *No, he told himself*, digging his fingernails into his palms. *I'm not going to cry.*

He felt a huge lump in his throat, and no matter how much he swallowed he couldn't loosen it. His vision grew watery as tears filled his eyes.

He felt humiliated, crying in front of her. She'd think he was a total baby. He doubled over, the teddy bear crushed on his lap, as he tried to hide his face. His shoulders shook from struggling to keep the sobs jammed inside his chest. But he knew she could see he was crying. No way to pretend he wasn't.

"This . . . this is stupid," he choked out. He took off his glasses and wiped his face. He stared at the wetness on his fingertips. "They're not even real, are they? I'm just imagining I'm crying."

"Mmm. I don't know," Death said. "They look like real tears to me." She settled back into the arm of the couch and tucked her feet up under her. "Why don't you tell me about this father thing."

"Do I have time to?" He'd never faced imminent death before. He didn't know how long it would take.

"We have time."

Tim wiped his face on his sleeve, then replaced his glasses. He cleared his throat a few times. "You're just trying to be nice. Thanks, but I don't need to talk. I'll be fine." He put the teddy bear between him and Death on the couch. He didn't want it to look like he was a little kid who needed a stuffed animal.

"Well, I'm not trying *not* to be nice, I'll grant you that. But I asked mainly because I'd like to know. What's this all about?"

Tim sighed. How could he possibly explain it all? He was still trying to understand it himself.

Tamlin sat beside Timothy Hunter's stiffening body. The boy was going blue, and his limbs twisted as the venom made its accursed way through his body.

The child has— Tamlin thought, then stopped himself. *What am I saying? "The child"? My son, I mean. My son has brought the land back from the dead. My son has broken a binding that Titania herself could not undo. He has overthrown an adversary no paladin of Faerie has ever dared challenge. And he has paid a grievous price. The manticore's venom seethes in his blood. And no healer born of woman ever worked a cure for that bane. He will die soon.*

Tamlin could not allow that to happen. He had to do something—anything. He stood over Tim and said words of transformation.

"Flesh of my flesh, be what you must if I am

to carry you," Tamlin said, tapping into the magic surrounding him, the magic of Faerie. "By our blood, breath of my breath, shape yourself as I will." With several passes of his hands, Tamlin felt the energies mingle and mix. The outline of the dying boy's body shimmered as he lost his human boundaries. The molecules and atoms rearranged themselves into a new shape, a shape Tamlin could work with.

Timothy Hunter transformed slowly into a hawk's feather. Once this was done, Tamlin, his father, assumed the hawk's shape. He picked up the quill of the feather in his beak, flapped his powerful wings, and took to the sky.

As Tamlin flew, he thought over the remarkable change in himself. *The boy was a stranger to me. For thirteen years of his life and three hundred of mine, I never gave him a thought. But now—*

Was it seeing him? Talking to him? Testing him? When did I begin to want to know him?

Tamlin traveled quickly, covering a great distance, urgency carrying him forward.

He saw into me. While I played at judging him, he needed no knife to cut to the heart of me. "Do you feel sorry for yourself all the time?" he asked me. And I struck him because he had seen and spoken a truth. I should have thanked him.

The infant he was—who I had never thought of

*again after that first moment—became a child whose
eyes pierce the darkness as mine never have and never
will. I would like to know the man that child will
become. Might have become.*

Upon reaching the palace gardens, Tamlin
swooped down and landed at the feet of Titania.
Laying the feather gently on the grass, he transformed himself back into human shape.

"Tamlin!" Titania cried. "Oh, Tam, you've
done it!" She flung her arms around his neck, her
body pressing against his. He could feel the life
flowing through her again, as it had when they
first met. Before it had all soured. Before the bindings. Before the manticore sucked the spirit from
the land. She was as restored as Faerie.

"Everything is beautiful again," she
exclaimed. "The garden is so alive. All the roses
are whispering secrets to one another." She ran
her hands along his arms and took both his hands
in hers. "Walk in the arbor with me, Tamlin. I
want you to hear them, too. You and no other."

Tamlin gently held her away from him. "I am
not the one who has restored your twilight land to
beauty. You owe me no thanks for your deliver-
ance. Another paid that price."

"Who did this, then?" Titania asked. "And
what is this price you speak of?"

Tamlin released Titania and faced Tim, still a

feather on the grass. Using his talents, Tamlin transformed Tim back into his twisted, pained, and suffering body. He stepped aside for Titania to see.

"Merciful gods," Titania gasped and dropped to her knees beside Tim's tortured body. "The child. Oh, Tamlin. The prophecies were true."

Tamlin gazed at his former love and watched her weep. She looked up at him, her eyes flashing with anger. "Who did this to him?" she demanded.

"The child was raving when I found him, lady. Delirious. But he gave me reason to believe he'd fought the manticore."

"The manticore," Titania repeated. "Tell me more."

Tamlin kneeled down beside her. "I brought the boy here for healing. Let the story wait."

"I have asked you once," Titania said, her voice stern. "Tell me what you know."

Why couldn't she just help? Why must she have the explanation? Perhaps, though, the explanation would give her the information she needed to help. "As you will," Tamlin acceded. "The withering of the land was the work of the manticore. The bindings you could not break were his. The child—"

"The *child*?" Titania repeated angrily. "He is called Timothy."

Tamlin was surprised at her vehemence, but if

she believed she had just cause, due to a misunderstood connection between herself and the boy, it would only work in his favor. His and the boy's.

"*Timothy* destroyed the manticore. How is anybody's guess. I found him wounded beyond my power to heal. So I flew him here to you."

Titania gazed sadly at the boy. "For the serpent's bite and the scorpion's sting, there are tinctures of great virtue. Against the breath of demons and the spittle of the mandrake, there are spells. But for the venom of the manticore, there is no cure. None, Tam. I am so sorry."

She stood and took Tamlin's hand. He did not shake her off. He knew she wanted to comfort him, and he wondered if comfort was possible. Beyond her, he could see that flowers were still blossoming, and creatures he had not seen in years fluttered or gamboled or frolicked in the lush grasses.

"I share your grief, Tamlin," Titania said. "But he was born to die, as they all are. The mortal blood in him—your blood—makes it so." She shook her head sadly. "It seems as though your kind barely live. They skim the surface of time and vanish without a ripple, like mayflies."

She released Tamlin's hand and stood over Tim again. "If only he had been raised in Faerie. The land and I would have worked our ways to blur those boundaries between your kind and mine."

This was not what Tamlin needed to hear—how things might have been different. *Things are as they are.*

Titania turned to face Tamlin. "Where did you say he slew the manticore?" she asked.

"Why?"

"You surprise me, Tamlin," Titania scolded. "Faerie lives because of Timothy's courage. We must honor his sacrifice. A monument will be built in the place of his victory. At the site of his triumph."

As Tamlin gazed down at his son's tortured, blue body, at the child who would not see manhood, he saw only waste. This may have been a victory for magic, for Faerie, and Tim may have triumphed over a monster, but how could Tamlin rejoice? Honor was a bitter achievement when one did not live to see it.

But he said none of this. He merely nodded, and lifted the boy into his arms. The boy who had done so much, when he, his father, had done so little.

Chapter Thirteen

DEATH WAS STILL WAITING. Tim hadn't spoken a word in some time. He decided there was no point in telling her his story. Why should he?

"Like you give a toss," he muttered. "Well, I'm sorry. I don't feel like relieving anyone's eternal boredom at the moment," he told her. He crossed his arms and stared straight ahead.

"Excuse me?" Death seemed startled. She stood up. "You don't want to talk to me? Fine. But I've got news for you, buster. I don't particularly enjoy being insulted." She picked up her mug and went over to the sink. She turned on the water and began washing dishes.

Tim instantly regretted his words. He hovered behind her at the sink. "Miss?" He still couldn't bring himself to call her "Death." "I didn't mean to upset you."

"Is that a fact?" She scrubbed a pot vigorously with a scouring pad.

"Well, yes . . . Yes, it is a fact."

Death turned off the faucet and dried her hands on a stained dishcloth. Ignoring Tim, she went over to a set of slatted double doors. Tim figured that it had originally been a pantry, but that she had converted it into a big walk-in closet. Tim was curious about what she might have stashed in there. He'd heard of a person having "skeletons in the closet." That would be singularly appropriate here. He fought back a giddy laugh.

"Stand back," Death instructed. She unlatched the double doors.

Tim did as he was told. He had no idea what might leap out at him from Death's closet.

Death ducked as an old toaster and a boot fell from a top shelf and nearly beaned her.

"Wow," Tim exclaimed. "That's the most packed, jammed closet I've ever seen."

"You should see the one in my bedroom," Death told him. "Now about your quest—you don't mind if I call it a quest, do you? I know you're touchy about certain words relating to magic."

"I don't mind," Tim assured her. "Are you still angry at me?" He continued to stare at the closet. He couldn't quite get over the amount of stuff in it. "Uh, are those all hats?"

"In the hatboxes? Nope. What's in them is

mostly junk." Death dropped down to a crouch and started shoving aside suitcases, file folders, and the hatboxes. She was obviously looking for something.

"I can't say that I'm angry at you, Mr. Sarcasm, but I haven't forgiven you either." She grunted as she pushed a box to the back of the closet. She glanced at Tim over her shoulder. "You might try apologizing. Works wonders."

"Oh. Sorry." He sat on the floor behind her. "I'm sorry."

"Apology accepted." She gave him one of her killer grins. *That's good*, Tim thought. *Death having a "killer grin." There were loads of opportunities for superbad puns in this situation*. Just the kind of jokes Molly punched him on the arm for but Tim knew she secretly enjoyed.

Death turned all the way around to face him directly. "Now as far as the quest thing goes— what are you really trying to find out?"

"I told you. I want to know who my father is. My real father."

"Uh-huh. You did say that. But you never said why."

"Why do you people have to make everything so complicated?" Tim complained.

"Hey, you were the one who said this was complicated, remember?" She turned back around and rummaged through the closet again. She seemed to have found what she'd been searching for; she tugged hard on a large trunk. "I'm just trying to figure out why someone as sensible as you would wander into a manticore's lair. I mean you didn't just wake up one morning suddenly dying to know whose gametes had the pleasure of becoming your blastocyst?"

"Huh?" *Now what language was she speaking?*

"Come on, you," she muttered to the trunk. She looked back at Tim. "You've had sex ed, right? You know. Sperm. Zygotes. Chromosomes, etcetera."

"Sure." *Man. More biology. Who knew school would ever turn out to be so important?*

She dragged the trunk all the way out of the closet. "Do you really care where your chromosomes came from?"

Tim's forehead wrinkled as he thought over her question. "I guess not."

"Well, what's the point of all this then?"

"I—I—I guess you know my mum is dead." *Oh, that's bloody brilliant*, Tim scolded himself. *Of course she knows that. She's Death.* He checked to see if she had caught that stupid remark. She was still just looking at him, her expression concerned.

"So it's just been me and Dad for a long

time," Tim explained. "He's okay, but he's . . . well, he sort of falls into himself sometimes, and he forgets I'm there. Then this homeless bloke told me that my real father was this really moody guy who can turn into a hawk. And this hawk guy, Tamlin, he's a falconer, whatever that is. The first time I met him, he hit me. The second time, he saved my life. So there's him, and there's my old dad, and I don't know which of them I belong to."

"Belong to?" Death repeated. "Ooooh, you people. Where do you get these ideas? You are so strange."

Death was poised on her hands and feet beside the open trunk. Her flashing black eyes bored right into Tim's. "Tim. Heredity is one thing. Identity is something else entirely. How on earth anyone could manage to confuse the two completely baffles me. But when you start talking about belonging to someone because they happened to be in the right place at the right time." She shook her head and sat back on her heels. "Oh, give me a break. If you belong to anyone, you belong to yourselves. And most of you never even manage that."

Tim's mouth dropped open. He had thought she was on his side. Now she seemed to be mocking him, putting him and everyone else down. His mouth clamped shut again.

You'd think being dead counted for some kindness, he thought.

Tamlin sat in the manticore's ruined estate. It was as if when Tim killed the beast anything that the manticore had touched exploded or shattered. The shelves of books were toppled, shards of glass from the display cases lay strewn about. Only the bones and preserved bodies of the manticore's collection remained. Some things are impossible to restore.

Once Titania had transported Tim and Tamlin to the mansion, Tamlin had cleared one of the large display pedestals. He found an elegant tapestry and covered the platform with it, then laid Tim's rigid body down on top of it. He placed candles at the four corners, creating a makeshift altar, then sank into a carved mahogany chair close by. He left the drapes drawn at the windows—he craved the darkness. He could not remember now how long ago his vigil had begun. Hours? Days?

Titania flung open the doors and stormed inside. "How much longer are you going to brood here, like an owl in the dark?" she asked. "Be done with tormenting yourself! Surely you do not blame yourself for the child's death."

"I see you now refer to Tim as 'the child,'" Tamlin noted. "And you speak as if he were already dead."

"Dead or alive, what is it to him that you sit here in the dark?" she admonished him. "Look into his eyes and you'll find only emptiness there. His spirit has flown."

She knelt beside Tamlin's thronelike chair and her voice became gentle. "Come away, Tamlin. We've lost Timothy, but we've found each other. It hurts me to see you caged here for days by your sorrow—lost as a hawk in a snare, so alone—when I am here for you." She placed her hand on his leg.

Tamlin shook off her hand as he stood. He had sat motionless for so long he felt stiff. "Not so long ago you said that I was not a man. A *hawk*, you called me."

"Tamlin, I—" Titania rose but made no move toward him. Tamlin could tell she was uncertain how to proceed. Well, so was he.

"You spoke in anger, but you spoke truth," he said. "I was young when you brought me here, lady. I learned hawk's shape and hawk's ways before I knew what it was to be a man. For six hundred years I've ridden the wind and hunted and called that life. Flown to your wrist when you wanted me there, and called that love." He felt anger welling up inside him. He turned to glare at her. "But it was a game, lady. Being your hawk. And I find I've tired of it."

Ignoring her stricken expression, he crossed to Tim. He placed his hands on the boy's cold forehead. Tim's body was quite blue now, and the skin was stretched taut against his bones, giving it a painfully skeletal appearance.

"It is not guilt that binds me to my son," Tamlin said. "The child that might have been ours. Nor is it grief. It is something you will never understand."

"Which is what?" Titania demanded behind him.

"Titania. May we have new candles, please? Two will do."

Tamlin stroked Tim's forehead, wishing to ease the boy's torment. There was a long pause.

"Candles," Titania said, her voice tight. "Very well."

Titania charged out of the mansion, fury and frustration coursing through her body. *He thinks I am his errand girl now?* She stopped when she reached the archway in the crumbled wall. "Amadan, attend me," she ordered.

The flitling appeared, hovering a few inches from her face. "No sooner said than done, my queen." He gave a little bow. "Now let your Fool

hear what's amiss. I've not seen you this angry
since yesterday." He grinned at her.

"Mind your tongue, jester, or expect to lose
it," Titania snapped. "What troubles me is none of
your affair."

She took in a calming breath, and conjured
herself at her most imperious. "Fetch two candles
and give them to the other fool—the one you'll
find communing with the corpse in there." She
waved at the mansion. "And should the encounter
suggest to you any amusing little songs or stories,
you will kindly refrain from repeating them to me,
unless you prefer to be voiceless the rest of your
days." With a snap of her fingers, Titania, Queen
of Faerie, vanished.

Poor little queen, Tamlin thought, as he
stroked Tim's twisted cheek. *It must be disconcert-
ing to find yourself jealous of a dying child. How
comforting it must be, at times like these, to know
that your world exists to console you.*

"Ahem."

Tamlin glanced over his shoulder. "Amadan,"
he greeted.

"I should have guessed these were for you,
Falconer." The flitling held up two candles as big
as his small body. "No one else has your knack for
infuriating queens," Amadan commented. "What a
special talent."

"Amadan. The candles."

Amadan flew to Tamlin and placed the candles alongside Tim. "So how have you put milady out of sorts this time? Did you slay the boy?"

Tamlin picked up one of the candle holders and removed the stubby remains of the burned-down candle. He replaced it with one of the new candles Amadan had delivered. "Amadan, I've been too busy to track you down. But if you will stay where you are just a moment longer, I'm sure that I can find the time to kill you."

Amadan fluttered away without another word.

Tamlin prepared the other candle. "It was Merlin who taught me the hawk's shape," he told Tim, even though he knew the child could not hear him. "He taught me much else besides. He wept in his wine as he told me how he stood beside Arthur's bed in Avalon, listening to the king moan, gripped in his death sleep."

Tamlin pulled several herbs from his sack and scattered them over Tim's body. "'I could heal him, he said in his withered old voice,'" Tamlin remembered. "'Why don't you then?' I had asked him, not believing him. 'You mock me,' Merlin replied, his eyes smoldering. He raised his hands and they turned to fire for a moment. I thought he meant to cast me into the fires of hell. Then he sank back into his chair and in a voice bitter with self-loathing said, 'No, you do not understand. How could you?' It was then that he told me of the spell."

Tamlin studied his handiwork. The herbs were in place, the candles were lit, the words recalled.

"Yes," Tamlin said. "The spell."

Chapter Fourteen

OKAY, NOW DEATH HAD REALLY ticked Tim off. "Oh, I'm so stupid," he retorted. "Us *people*, we're all so bloody stupid. Right. Thanks, then." Tim stood up, but realized he had nowhere to go.

Death flipped open the lid of the trunk and started taking things out. A bag of nails. A stack of postcards. Mismatched socks. "I wish you'd stop putting words into my mouth. I don't think you're stupid. Not you in particular anyway. Just confused."

"Easy for you to say," Tim muttered.

"Yep. It is."

She continued rummaging. It infuriated Tim. She was so casual. This was big stuff to him. Didn't she get it?

"*You* don't have to worry about anything," he said in an accusing tone.

"Nope. I don't. Oh, look! I found it!" She held

up an envelope and grinned.

Tim didn't care what she had found. She didn't seem to be paying attention to what he was saying. She was more concerned about that stupid little envelope than she was about him.

"Nobody can make you do anything you don't want to. Not adults, not fairies—nobody!" Tim complained. "And you can't get lost, and you know what you're doing and stuff. You have your weird mission." He shook his head and glared at her. "You're so happy, it's bizarre."

"Weird mission?" She laughed. "That's pretty good." Finally her expression grew more serious and she looked straight at him. "Tim," she said, "everything you said is true. Maybe you should ask yourself—" She cut herself off and looked as if she were hearing something in the distance. "Oops, too late. Sorry, Tim. It's weird mission time."

Tim gaped at her. She was just about to tell him something important and she was leaving? "B-b-b-but—it's not fair!" he sputtered.

"You're right," she agreed. "It's not."

Tim collapsed as everything went all black and swirly again.

The pain, Tamlin thought. *It is only pain. Soon it will end. The death he would have died is mine now*. Tamlin moaned in agony, writhing in his thronelike chair. *When the sacrifice is done, my life will be his.*

"Tamlin?" Death appeared in front of him. "You can let go now."

Her voice was gentle and true, the tones bell-like. Tamlin felt himself rise out of his body and go to her.

"Lady? Will the child be—"

"Oh, Tim will be fine," the woman assured him. She cocked her head to one side. "It's too bad the two of you couldn't talk a while, though. There was something he wanted to ask you."

Tamlin gazed down on his son. Already, the life Tamlin had sacrificed was now reanimating the boy. Tim's limbs untwisted, color returning to his skin.

"Must we leave him here to face Titania alone?" Tamlin turned back to the girl he knew to be the angel of death. "Titania believes she loves me and she will blame him for my death. She will be vicious. Cruel."

"Tim will handle it," Death said. "You'd be surprised at that boy's resources. Let's go."

Tamlin nodded, and then they were gone.

Tim stirred. His movement toppled a candle, dripping hot wax on his hands. "Ouch!" he exclaimed. He sat up and took in his surroundings, confused. "Huh? If this is supposed to be my funeral, someone's going to be disappointed."

He swung his legs over the side of the platform he was laid out upon and dropped to the floor. "How did I get back to this place?" he wondered as he gazed around the manticore's mansion. "Someone should recommend a good maid service," he commented, kicking aside some broken glass.

Now I just have to remember where the door is, Tim thought as he made his way through the mess. He froze when he saw the twisted figure in the thronelike chair.

His heart thudded. He recognized that leather gauntlet, that long hair. Suddenly he realized what must have happened.

"You jerk!" Tim shouted. He stumbled to Tamlin's twisted, dead body. "Why did you do it? I was dying just fine and you had to go and butt in."

He sank down beside the chair and wept. Hard, rasping sobs racked his body in waves. He felt for the Opening Stone Tamlin had given him, and he cried for his dad in London and for this father he had just discovered, who had sacrificed himself for him. For all of his own confusion, and sorrow, and exhaustion.

Finally, depleted, raw, he wiped his face with his T-shirt. He leaned against the chair and hugged himself. He felt so cold. Tim felt as if he knew even less now. Understood nothing at all. All he could think was how much he wanted to see Molly. He shut his eyes, still holding the stone, and fell into sleep, exhausted.

When he awoke again, he was back in his room in London and the phone was ringing. The Opening Stone was still in his hand.

Disoriented, he automatically picked up the receiver. "Hello?" he said, his voice rough and hoarse.

"Tim?" Molly said. "Are you okay?"

"What?"

"Did you talk to your dad yet?" she asked. "About, you know, what we talked about a little while ago?"

"When?" He knew he sounded like a right idiot, but she was confusing him. Wasn't his conversation with her days ago?

"Tim, what's going on? You seemed sort of all right when you left here an hour ago. Now you sound shook up again. What did your dad say to you?"

An hour ago? Then Tim remembered that time went all funny in magical realms.

"You promised to ring me after you talked to your dad. Have you done it yet?"

"Yes," he said. "Yes, I've talked to him. Sorry

not to have gotten back to you—I got a little caught up in something."

"So is it true?" Molly asked.

"Yes, I suppose it is," Tim replied. He put a hand in his pocket, and his fingers wrapped around something that felt like paper. He pulled a small envelope out of his pocket. Tim stared at it. "What's this?"

"What's what?" Molly asked.

"Nothing," Tim said. He opened the envelope that he realized he had last seen in Death's apartment. The thing she'd been looking for. For some reason, she had given it to him. He poured out the contents into his hand. They looked like seeds. *How weird*.

"Listen, I think I should probably go now," Tim said.

"Do you want to come over?" she offered. "I could make you some tea. Mum swears it has calming effects."

He did want to see her, but there was something he wanted to do, and he figured he should do it alone. "Nah. It's late. Your parents would freak if I showed up now. Oh—and Molly?" he added. "To make a really good cup of tea, don't let the water boil too long."

Molly laughed. It was a nice laugh. "Well, expert, I'll be sure to ask your advice on all cooking

matters." Then her voice grew soft. "If you want
to ring back . . . no matter how late . . ."

"Thanks, Molly. I'm okay now." And he
almost felt as if that were true.

They hung up. Tim stared at the seeds lying
on his palm. Closing his hand around them, he tip-
toed out of the house. All of the lights were out.
His dad must have already gone to bed.

The streets were dark and cold, but Tim
barely felt it. He moved quickly, sticking to the
shadows, because the dark was where he felt
stronger right now. He covered ground quickly
and finally arrived at the cemetery.

Never letting go of the seeds, he hoisted himself up and over the gate. He dropped onto the icy
dirt and crept toward the familiar little mound.

He knelt at his mother's grave and gazed at her
tombstone. "Hey, Mum. I really wish you could tell
me how this all happened. But I guess it doesn't
really matter now, does it? You're gone. Tamlin
is gone. But I'm still here. And no matter how it
happened, you meeting up with a man who is also
a hawk, I mean, well, I guess I'm still me. Nothing
changes that."

Tim cleared a spot of dirt on top of his mother's
resting place. He dug a shallow hole and sprinkled
the seeds into it before covering them up.

He sat a moment longer, enjoying the dark

night, enjoying the feeling of being alive. Then he stood on much steadier legs than he'd had when he arrived. "Good-bye," he said to the tombstone. "For now."

He left the cemetery without a backward glance. Still, he couldn't help wondering as he made his way back home in the dark, what he had just planted. What would grow from those seeds?

And what would become of all of his new knowledge? And new questions? Discovering that your dad wasn't really your dad, what impact would that have—on both of them? And knowing that his real father had sacrificed himself so that Tim might live . . . Tim shook his head. How was he ever going to process that one?

Tim turned a corner, and the angle of a street-lamp illuminated his reflection in a darkened store window. He stopped and stared at himself.

"So, Timothy Hunter, who are you?" he asked himself. "That's okay, go all closemouthed," he teased his reflection. "Or are you just keeping things close to the vest? Probably a good idea in these strange times." He grinned. "Maybe you're not as dumb as you look, Hunter."

Hunter. Tim realized that his last name was Hunter only because his mother had married Mr. Hunter. If she'd married Tamlin, Tim's name would be . . . what?

It dawned on him. Timothy Hunter, then, couldn't be his "true" name. It _was_ just what he was "called."

So what _was_ his real name?

"No, thank you," he told his reflection. "I've had enough of questions for the time being."

He headed home. For once, he let his mind empty and simply enjoyed the fact that the cold air reminded him that he had lungs, and that the night sky was full of stars, and that somehow, he had saved an entire world.

The journey continues in
The Books of Magic 3:
THE CHILDREN'S CRUSADE

THE YEAR WAS 1212. *The fourth crusade had come to a bloody end. The result had been every bit as successful as the previous three, which is to say it had been a complete and utter failure. For over a hundred years, armies had marched on the holy city, but Jerusalem was still in the hands of the Saracens.*

Then a man in the garb of a holy monk rose up among the people of France and Germany. He preached a dark gospel to them all.

"Why have all the crusades failed?" he demanded. "Even with the might and love and power of God on our side, why do our armies always fall to the heathens? Why?"

His dark eyes flashed at the stunned and silent crowd. "Because we are not pure!" he answered for them. His voice thundered with the timbre of the righteous. "Because our soldiers are already soiled and stained with sin. How can we sinners win for ourselves the Holy Land?" He paused, letting the sinners before him contemplate the question. "How? I tell you how! We must raise an army of innocents. An army of children. And when they reach Jerusalem, with God

*and innocence on their side, our victory shall be
assured. This will be the greatest of all of the holy
wars. This will be the Children's Crusade!"*

The crowd murmured and mumbled and slowly
dispersed. He had held them enthralled until he pro-
nounced his solution; after that they dismissed him.
But they spoke of him and his mad plan.

The words of the monk were transmitted across
Europe. Adults scoffed, but the children heard—and
believed. Throughout the continent children huddled
together, whispering, planning, thinking, yearning.
They flocked to the crusade. Some left their parents
and their comfortable homes. Others left alleys,
farms, and forests.

Over fifty thousand boys and girls traveled to
Marseilles, where one hundred ships waited for them.
None of the children knew where Jerusalem was, nor
what would happen when they got there, but their
faith sustained them. The man dressed as the monk
stood at the docks and watched the children board the
ships. And he smiled.

The ships set sail in January 1213. Over the
next few months, children continued to arrive in
Marseilles, hoping to join the crusade. But once those
one hundred ships had set sail, none were to follow.
The late arrivals wept at the shore, heartbroken that
they could not be part of the army of God.

They were the lucky ones.

A great storm came up and destroyed ninety-eight of the hundred ships. Forty-nine thousand children drowned that night. It could be argued that they, too, were the lucky ones. For the hundred ships were not bound for Jerusalem but for the port of Anfa in Morocco. And the children were not to be the champions of a holy war but chattel in a thriving slave trade.

The remaining two ships arrived in Morocco and were met by a smiling man who was no longer dressed as a monk. Eight hundred children (two hundred had died during passage) were unloaded and sold in the port marketplace. Word of the children's fate slowly trickled back to Europe. The identity of the monk who began the affair was never discovered.

Fifty thousand children departed for the crusade. None of them ever returned home.

Aiken Drum and his sister, Mwyfany, marched across the burning sands. They had survived the storms, but they were now in a strange land. They had traveled so far for so long; Aiken could no longer remember how long. First there had been the excitement of joining the Crusade. They were to do great things! They were going to become important, a part of something so much larger than themselves. This excitement and purpose propelled them to Marseilles, and their faith was what sustained them once on board the ship.

Aiken and his sister knew no fear at first. And even as the great ship lurched and rolled, even as they shivered together, imagining the horrors that the war they were about to join might bring, they remained brave, for they knew they were on the side of all that was good and right and true. Their God would protect them. After all, it was for Him and His glory that they had undertaken this great journey. If their treatment by the crew was rough, or indifferent at best, the eager children thought nothing of it. Taking care of the ship was far more important than taking care of them, they reasoned.

That was before the others drowned. And before their own arrival in Morocco.

They had been sold, like the rest of the remaining survivors of the voyage, in the clamor of the marketplace. Mwyfany had cowered against him, frightened by the words shouted at them in strange languages, the pungent aromas, and peculiar wares. At first, Aiken counted himself lucky that he and Mwyfany had not been separated. But now he wondered if she would have been better off sold to a different master.

How long would this forced march go on? he wondered again and again as the sand scraped the bottom of his feet and the sun made his eyes burn.

"Aiken!" Mwyfany called.

Aiken twisted to see his sister, the ropes chafing at his wrists. She had fallen and was struggling to stand up. Her efforts were dragging down the children around her. The captors released her from the ropes that tied her to the others. She still could not stand. The captors cracked a whip to keep the line moving. They left her where she was, digging at the sand, trying to get up.

"No!" Aiken cried. He dug in his heels and stopped. One of the men whipped him, and for good measure whipped the boy in front of him and the girl behind, making sure they kept picking up their feet.

"Mwyfany!" Aiken cried. "Mwyfany!"

The stinging whip, the searing sand, and his own weakened body betrayed him. All conspired to keep him from stopping for her, from fighting. He could not even say a prayer—or a good-bye.

The tears he cried for his sister trickled down his dirty cheeks, but he made no sound. His body shuddered as he struggled to keep the racking sobs from exploding out of him.

He felt a soft touch on his back, and his head whipped around. Gazing into the dark eyes of the girl behind him, Aiken saw sympathy and sorrow.

On and on. On and on. They traveled across the desert and then by water, then across a forest. Late one starless night, they came to a city and were led through dark streets into a huge building. Once inside, they were pushed down into a cellar and were left there in the dark.

There were twelve of them now: twelve exhausted, filthy, frightened, starving children. None was over the age of fourteen.

Slowly, they edged their way into understanding one another—a few words of French, English, Italian, or Spanish here and there. Some of the boys spoke a little Latin. Eventually, with this strange amalgam of languages they created a new one of their own design. They whispered together, offering comfort, and wondered about their fate.

Aiken learned that the dark-eyed girl was named Yolande and that she had come from Spain with her sister. She didn't tell him why she was alone now; she didn't have to. Her braids were matted, and her face was thin and haggard from the journey. He guessed her to be about ten years old—just midway between his age and Mwyfany's—but their ordeal had given her the look of a wizened old creature. He supposed he must look far older than his own fourteen years.

It was impossible to tell what was day and what was night in the pit. From time to time the trapdoor opened and someone threw down rotten meat or spoiled fruit. Water was lowered in a bucket once a day. And as time passed, the smell in the pit grew worse and worse. They lived in the dark, and never knew how much time was passing.

Then one day some men came down and took Yolande away.

Aiken sat in the pit, his back against the slimy wall, and listened with the others. Yolande's screams sent chills along his spine. And then came sudden silence, which was even worse. The children looked at one another in the little bit of light that made its way into the cellar, acknowledging with growing horror that they now knew their futures.

Somehow, maybe in response to his terror, Aiken fell asleep. He hadn't even begun to dream when he awoke with a start. Yolande stood before him, speaking in his own language, though she had never learned more than a few words of it. "There is a way out," she told him. "There is a place to go, where you will always be safe." And then she showed him how.

He blinked, and she was gone. He peered into the darkness and saw shining wide-awake eyes all around him. Yolande had appeared to them all and had spoken to each in his native tongue.

"A gate," she had promised them. And now they knew how to open it.

"We'll do it now," Aiken said in the language they had created. Nods went around the circle.

"We should have a leader," someone said.

How to choose? This was not a time for making speeches or taking votes. The simplest methods are always the best. Around the circle they went, playing rock, paper, scissors, eliminating a player with each turn. Finally it came down to the boy named Kerwyn. He was the oldest, a little older than Aiken.

They settled into a circle, and Kerwyn took his knife and cut each child's finger. They used this blood to draw the special pattern Yolande had described on the floor. Sometimes Kerwyn had to cut the children more than once in order to have enough blood. Creating this door to freedom had its cost. They were the first; they had to give of themselves to break through. And the ritual bound them together as blood brothers and sisters.

Finally, they were ready. Kerwyn was the first to dance the pattern. The hopscotch grid glowed crimson—and he vanished! It had worked!

Aiken thought of his sister. If only . . . He shook his head. It was too late now for wishing. One by one, the children hopped the pattern and disappeared. Aiken approached the hopscotch grid. He took a deep breath and jumped . . .

. . . into Free Country. Where nothing could ever hurt them again.